OF SONS A.

# OF SONS AND STARS

*Short stories by*

CATHERINE MERRIMAN

honno
*MODERN FICTION*

*Published by Honno*
*'Alisa Craig', Heol y Cawl, Dinas Powys*
*Bro Morgannwg, Wales, CF64 4AH*

*First Impression 1997*

© *Catherine Merriman 1997*

**British Library Cataloguing in Publication Data**

A catalogue record for this book is available from the British Library

ISBN 1 870206 27 4

*Published with the financial support of the Arts Council of Wales*

Cover design by Debbie Maidment

Typeset and printed in Wales by
Gwasg Dinefwr, Llandybïe

# Contents

# *Acknowledgements*

The following stories in this collection have already been broadcast or have appeared in print:

'The Last Thirty-Nine-Year-Old Housewife' in *New England Review* and on Radio 4; 'Seducing Him' in *The Interpreter's House*; 'Of Sons and Stars' in *Essentials Magazine, Avantage*; 'Mustard' in *Luminous and Forlorn* (Honno, 1994); 'Slideshow' in *Essentials Magazine*; 'The Rules of a Man's Life' in *You Magazine* and on Radio 4; 'Blue Pastel Woman' in *Intimate Portraits* (Seren); 'The Special Day' in *New England Review, Essentials Magazine*; 'Learning to Speak Klingon' in *Planet*.

# THE LAST THIRTY-NINE-YEAR-OLD HOUSEWIFE

Judith was undressing on Friday night in front of her long bedroom mirror when she realized – with a shock that momentarily paralyzed her – that she had become invisible. There, behind her – or rather where her reflection should have been – was the vivid paisley of the duvet on the neatly-made kingsize bed. There, to the right, was the angled view of her highly polished dressing table, and on it her make-up bag, jewellery box, brush and comb. And at her feet – or where the image of her feet should have been – was the soft grey pile of the newly vacuumed carpet. But she – she was nowhere.

Shock gave way, slowly, to sinking comprehension. She should have guessed. She had detected a curious sensation – creeping nothingness, she now realized – in the car, driving back from the pub. In fact, hadn't it started earlier? About nine-thirty, at that kick-in-the-guts moments after Suzanne had arrived, late as usual, and bursting with pride and achievement.

Judith crossed the room and climbed into bed. Drearily she thought: I am an anachronism. A dinosaur. The last thirty-nine-year-old housewife. Once there were six of us.

Six friends with young children, six mothers, six wives. We've stayed friends, and we still meet every Friday night, but that's all. Four of us, since last summer, back at work. Suzanne and I were the last, and now I'm on my own. Her children are younger than mine, but she's not a mother any more. She's not a wife any more. She's a civil servant. And what am I? Andrew is fifteen. Florence is thirteen. I have been married seventeen years. I'm still a wife, and a mother, and now I'm invisible.

Her husband Denis entered the bedroom. Of course, he could see her. Judith knew that her nothingness was a personal revelation, not a supernatural event.

She watched Denis get undressed, also in front of the long mirror. After removing his check shirt he stood sideways to his clear, confident reflection, sucked his stomach in, and patted his belly flesh. Judith saw the image in the mirror grin, a friendly, satisfied smile.

'D'you think I should get a job?' she asked.

Without altering the direction of his gaze Denis said, 'You've got one.'

He was referring to her three mornings running the village playgroup. She watched him move away from the mirror.

'A proper job,' she said, treacherously.

'What's brought this on?' Denis flung his trousers onto a chair. He smiled back at her.

Judith thought. She tried to look behind Suzanne's announcement, and her own sudden nothingness.

'I'm not sure,' she said. Was it envy? Guilt? Fear of missing out? Being left behind?

Denis climbed into bed beside her. Automatically she shifted her body towards his, and automatically he slipped his arm around her shoulders. They lay side by side, staring up at the ceiling.

'Aren't you happy?' Denis asked. 'I thought you were.'

'I don't know,' said Judith.

'Well,' said Denis. 'If you did work, what would you like to do?'

'I don't know,' said Judith again. 'It's been so long. I don't know what I'm good at.'

There was a silence. Finally, sounding comfortable and relaxed, Denis said, 'Well, I don't mind. It's up to you, really, isn't it.'

'I suppose so,' said Judith in a small voice, though she wasn't at all sure it was.


The following day, Saturday, the morning was too busy for Judith to ponder long on her nothingness, though it was still apparent – or rather, conclusively non-apparent – in the bedroom, and indeed bathroom, mirror.

After breakfast, because Florence asked her graciously, she helped her daughter tidy her bedroom. 'Helped' turned out to be the wrong word. Judith was guiltily aware, as she scrabbled beneath desk and dressing table for scattered make-up brushes, felt-tip pens, teaspoons, and grungy screws of tissues, that she was doing all the work. Florence had lost interest and was sprawled on her bed rereading an old copy of *Smash Hits*. But Judith had the mess firmly by the throat by then, and it was such a satisfying room to tidy. She began to feel almost cheerful. I'm good at this, she thought, I even enjoy it. I could be a Professional Tidier.

She stood up with an armful of rubbish and dumped it in the bin beneath her daughter's pin-up-encrusted mirror. She straightened, facing the mirror.

'Good grief,' she said. There, encircled by the sinister images of long-haired and leather-clad young men, a pathetic creature stared out. A skivvy, instantly recognizable from the headscarf and hairpins and floral pinny. Judith stared at her, appalled.

The image disappeared. Judith controlled the tremble in
her throat. She felt a well of anger and turned accusingly to
Florence. Had she done this? But Florence was still deep in
her magazine. Judith touched her head, checking, and fled
from the room.

She made a cheese soufflé for lunch. Cooking always had
a calming effect on her. It was just a hallucination, she told
herself, as she grated the cheese. I was skivvying for Florence
and feeling guilty about it. A mental projection.

She separated the eggs, feeling more relaxed already. I'm
good at cooking, she thought. And I like it. Maybe I could
be a Chef. Watching the butter melt in the pan she contemplated the challenge of cooking for dozens, maybe even
hundreds. Would mass production be quite as enjoyable?

There was an odd white blemish on the polished alu-
minium strip above the cooker controls. She brushed a hand
over it, before realizing that it was some sort of reflection. It
was moving with her. She stood on tiptoe and saw her forehead and eyes appear, beneath the white. Then she bent her
knees, dipping down. She was wearing a white hat. A very
tall white hat, with – gracious, how appropriate – a soufflé
crown.

She pulled the saucepan off the heat while she caught her
breath. All right. Just another hallucination. She glanced at
the cooker. The white mark had gone. She exhaled deeply,
and pushed the pan back onto the ring.

Denis, used to bread and lump cheddar for Saturday
lunch, said, 'Hey, terrific,' when she called him in from the
garden. He and Andrew had been lifting turf from the corner
of the lawn where they were digging Judith a small pond.
Florence announced to Denis that she'd tidied her bedroom
and Judith smiled grimly but didn't contradict her.

After lunch Andrew asked if someone would drive him
into town so he could buy a new computer game.

'Take the bus,' said Denis. 'I want to get your mother's pond dug.'

'Oh please,' moaned Andrew. He turned to Judith. 'Mum, please.'

Judith took pity on the boy – the bus fare would take a quarter of his pocket money – and agreed to take him. She liked driving the car anyway – it was much more powerful and fun than the last they'd had. She and Andrew left straight after lunch. As she adjusted the bucket seat and strapped herself in she glanced at the driving mirror and thought she detected, above the hazy blankness that should have been her face, a chauffeur's peaked cap. Oh God, she sighed to herself.

In town, while waiting for Andrew to return from the computer shop, she bought a congratulations card for her friend Suzanne. Of course I mean it, she thought, suppressing the ache that gnawed at her as she waited to pay for it. She signed and stamped the card hastily, and posted it on the way to Boots. There she bought a small make-up mirror in a black plastic sleeve. Interestingly, while selecting the mirror, she was able to see her face in it, looking quite normal: a trifle anxious and harassed, she thought, and perhaps more stupid than she would have hoped. But recognizably herself. At the checkout it came to her. Of course, I'm a consumer, she thought wearily. I exist as a consumer …

When they got home the hole in the lawn was more than two feet deep. Denis had the black polythene liner spread out on the grass nearby and was waiting for her to approve the final shape. Judith had been anticipating this moment for weeks; she forgot about personal nothingness, and the mirror, and who she was, or wasn't, and simply enjoyed the rest of the day.

The following morning, however – Sunday – she was still invisible. Today the family were making their monthly visit to Judith's parents and, as Judith was putting on her coat for the journey, she discovered in the pocket the little mirror she'd bought in town. She told Denis he could drive, slipped the mirror out of its cover, and at intervals during the forty-mile journey glanced surreptitiously into it. At the start of the journey she was a blurry nothingness; by the end she was clear and solid, with blonde pigtails, a sweet snub nose, and clearly aged around twelve.

All the same, it wasn't unenjoyable, being treated as a child. She let her father fuss over her with drinks before lunch, and gave her mother the usual update of family events, editing out those parts she knew her mother wouldn't want to hear, and glossing up those she knew she would enjoy. So the fact that Andrew had got drunk on cider with his friends and thrown up on his bedroom carpet didn't get mentioned, but Florence's top marks for her history project did. Judith had actually brought the folder with them and, sitting on a footstool beside her mother, knew she was glowing with as much pride at her daughter's achievement as if she had done the work herself.

After a roast lamb lunch Denis and Judith's father, armed with ladders, went out the front to lop branches overhanging the front drive. Judith's mother had her Sunday nap, while Judith played badminton with the children on the back lawn. As she whooped and panted beside Florence she thought: what a contented, united, successful family we appear when we're here. She smiled wryly, suddenly rechristening the children Janet and John, and imagining Denis up his ladder with a pipe welded between his teeth. But the picture didn't seem fraudulent – just funny. I'm a good daughter, she sighed to herself; I live up, and down, to my parent's expectations. I don't burden them with things they wouldn't understand, or would hurt them, or they can't help with. I bring our little triumphs over for their approval, and let them indulge us. And I don't mind any of it. She grinned to herself: even pigtails quite suit me.

She drove on the late journey home. Half-way back Florence, who had drunk wine during the day and was consequently overtired, picked a fight with Andrew. She accused him of taping over one of her videos. Andrew told her that if she was stupid enough not to label tapes, then tough. The argument became mildly physical. Judith could feel Florence's knees jabbing into her back. Denis, infuriatingly, merely turned the radio volume up.

Judith pulled in at a lay-by, switched off the radio, and swung round.

'Will you two behave,' she snapped. 'Florence, you're behaving like a two-year-old. Why d'you have to bring this up now? It must have happened days ago. I'm trying to drive. Just sit still and shut up.'

'You always take Andrew's side,' Florence shouted. 'I hate you,' and she burst noisily into tears.

They had to listen to her forcing out sobs for the rest of the journey. On their way into the house Judith said, 'Come on, dear, you're tired,' and tried to put a forgiving arm around the girl, but was pushed away. 'Leave me alone,' Florence hissed, and pounded upstairs. The slam of her bedroom door shook the house.

Judith's patience snapped. She crashed into the bathroom furious with everyone: with Florence for being such a self-centred little bitch, with Andrew for his complacent sniggers, and with Denis for sitting, as usual, on his edge-of-battleground fence.

'Little cow,' she seethed, snatching up her toothbrush and the toothpaste. She started to clean her teeth in the mirror. God, I look ugly when I'm cross, she thought and, suddenly alarmed, removed the brush from her mouth. Were those warts on her nose? Warts? My God … and was that … Christ, she was wearing a pointy black hat …

She flung the toothbrush down and, trembling, rinsed her face and patted it dry.

Denis came in and put his arms around her from behind. 'Don't get upset,' he murmured. 'You mustn't let her wind you up.'

'Ha!' said Judith, shrugging him off. 'Easy for you, isn't it? You're not the one with the broomstick.'

'Eh?' said Denis. 'Who said anything about sticks? We're not talking corporal punishment, surely?'

'Oh shut up,' said Judith, and stormed off to the bedroom.


In the morning, however, the atmosphere cleared. Florence appeared promptly for breakfast and although she didn't actually apologize, said, 'Mmm, great Mum,' as she was handed a perfectly ordinary slice of toast and, unusually, kissed Judith before leaving for the school bus. Judith returned the kiss warmly.

It was one of Judith's playschool mornings and she was down at the village hall before nine. She had twenty-two children in her charge – the entire preschool population of the village. It was a matter of pride to Judith that there wasn't a local child under thirteen whom she hadn't had, at least briefly, in her care. Not one child whose development she hadn't added to, in some way.

Today there was a new enrolment, a plump red-faced little girl from the starter homes at the edge of the village. Judith took her by the hand and led her and her young mother around the busy hall, introducing them to the activities: the sandpit, the climbing frame, the dressing-up corner, the water bath. She explained the function and importance of each and as usual found her own words inspiring. The years between two and four were special, crucial years. Of course they were. And rewarding. The children were, in the main, lovable, and even the unlovable few were less so by the time she sent them up to school.

Her morale high, she introduced the new mother to one of her adult helpers and left them chatting. The little girl was already happily settled in the playhouse. Then she marched two of her small boys, whose bladders were inclined to leak, to the lavatories. She steered them into the cubicles.

As she stood back she caught sight of herself in the large blistered mirror over the handbasins. She clutched at her chest. What enormous breasts! Heavens, she was huge, cowlike! And what was she wearing? A multicoloured tent? She looked like a relic from the sixties.

Suddenly furious – she had been feeling good, dammit – she hoiked the two little boys out of the cubicles and bustled them back to the hall. But the morning was spoilt. Even at story time, the ten minutes she usually enjoyed most, she felt resentful, undermined. A rainbow smock, for goodness' sake. She'd looked idiotic. Was that really how people saw her?

She plodded home at twelve-thirty and, feeling rebellious, defrosted a chocolate cheesecake in the microwave and scoffed half of it for lunch. She noted with satisfaction the dozen or so chemicals listed on the packet. The other half of the cake she earmarked, as an act of maternal irresponsibility, for the children's tea.

Andrew came home from school at four complaining of a sore throat.

'Really sore,' he insisted. 'I couldn't eat any chips at lunch time.'

'Oh dear,' sighed Judith, feeling herself slotting back into duty. She found a torch, sat him down, and told him to say *aah*.

'Can't see much,' she said. She detected disappointment in the boy's face and added, 'Maybe it looks a little red.'

'Honestly,' said Andrew, sounding peeved. 'It really does hurt.'

'I'm sure it does,' Judith said soothingly, and stuck a thermometer in his mouth. With his lips pursed around the glass the boy's eyes looked huge and mournful. Judith felt a mushy wave of tenderness for him and knew without looking that her head had just sprouted a crisp white cap, adorned with a red cross.

Andrew's temperature was normal. She shook the mercury down and said kindly, 'We'll see how it is later, OK?'

Despite Andrew's throat and lingering playschool memories, Judith had a good evening. Florence returned from school still in a generous mood and Denis came home with a bottle of wine and a damp sackful of plants for the empty pond. After supper they attached the hose and watched the water creep up the black plastic, toasting the level at intervals with the red wine. The pond wasn't full until after dark so they put the plants in the shed for Judith to deal with the next day.

She and Denis went to bed that night feeling deeply affectionate. Judith left her nightie off and Denis said, 'Mmm, you're lovely,' as he snuggled up to her.

Between kisses, Judith noticed the little make-up mirror that she'd left lying on the bedside table. As Denis lay across her, nuzzling her earlobe, a whim made her reach out for it. She held it behind his head.

'What *are* you doing?' Denis asked.

'It's meant to make it more exciting,' Judith improvised.

'Really?' Denis sounded baffled, but not discouraging. 'Isn't it a little small?'

Judith didn't reply, because she had just found her face in the glass. It must have been the dim bedroom lighting that made the image so soft and rosy. But was she really still so blonde? Surely not. She gazed at the image for a moment, entranced, then put the mirror aside. Astonishing. She didn't know whether to be gratified, or affronted.

'I'm not a sex kitten,' she said, but with a rush of emotion that made her tighten her arms around Denis's back.

'Absolutely not,' Denis mumbled, kissing her chin, her neck, her shoulder.

Judith gave up thinking for half an hour. Afterwards, feeling genuinely soft and rosy, she lay staring up into the blackness. Denis was on his front beside her, already asleep, his arm resting heavily across her stomach.

Calmly she thought: I am thirty-nine years old and I am in a panic. To my daughter I am apparently a witch or a skivvy. To my son, a chauffeur and a nurse. To my husband – among other things, I hope – a sex kitten. To my parents, a little girl. In town I am a harassed consumer and at play-group a ridiculous earth mother ...

She blinked into the darkness, feeling the images roll themselves into a huge dull-coloured weight, pressing down on her chest. She exhaled a sigh, and felt the weight tremble. Slowly she started again.

I am thirty-nine years old ... and I am in a panic. In the company of my daughter I see myself as a witch and a skivvy ...

A dent seemed to form in the huge weight. It deepened to a hole. There was something warm and soft, glowing inside. She started again.

I am in a panic ... why? Because ... I am thirty-nine. Because all my friends are going out to work. And I'm not. Because I'm frightened of being left behind. Because I'm worried that I should be doing something more with my life. Because I'm frightened that I am not fulfilling myself. Not fulfilling some duty to myself ... To myself.

The weight imploded, disappearing into the warm hole. And then she yawned, suddenly very sleepy.

In the morning she threw on her jeans and a sweatshirt – it was another playschool morning – and strode into her daughter's bedroom. Florence was half-dressed, peering at her face in the dressing-table mirror.

Judith leant over her aggressively. 'Do you see me as a witch and a skivvy?'

'I see you as a large boring object blocking my light,' said Florence good-naturedly. 'Move, Mum, will you.'

'I never wore make-up when I was thirteen,' Judith sniffed. She marched to her son's bedroom.

Andrew was propped up invalid-like on the pillows. He had his mouth open before she had released the door latch.

'Iss awhul,' he croaked.

'Am I a nurse?' she asked, coming firmly into the room. 'Is that how you see me? Or a chauffeur?' She squinted into his mouth. 'No.' She frowned and felt his neck. 'Maybe a telephonist. I'll call the doctor.'

She left Andrew visibly brightened and walked back towards her own bedroom. Outside the bathroom door she stopped. From here she could see Denis sitting on the edge of their bed, pulling on his socks. She could hear Florence's voice, singing along to rock music on the radio. Behind her Andrew gave a series of pathetic coughs. She stood completely still, and for a glorious moment saw herself, quite distinctly, at the centre of the universe. She felt the tug and check of the bodies orbiting around her. Even the inanimate bodies: the house, the garden, the pond. And then the minor satellites beyond: her playgroup babies, women friends, relatives, the whole known world really, all distantly circling, their faces towards her.

She hurried into her bedroom.

'I think Andrew has tonsillitis. I'll ring the doctor before I go to playgroup and ask if I can take him down to the surgery at lunch-time. This afternoon I will make a beef carbonade for supper, do a little ironing, and spend as long as possible planting the pond and gloating over it.'

'OK,' said Denis.

Judith snatched up the little mirror from the bedside table, walked out of the bedroom to the top of the stairs, and dropped it, mirror side down, over the banister. She watched it fall and shatter to smithereens on the parquet floor below.

That was silly of me, she thought, and went down to get a dustpan and brush.

# HOG ROAST

A moment ago it was that stomping-around, half busy, half sensible time before a party. Now the Wraiths and the Dragons have arrived together in a roar of bikes – more than a dozen, plus a couple of small vans – and suddenly it's chaos. Tom the landlord, who's lent us the Talywain for the evening, has come out to watch. Arms folded firm across his chest, eyes steady – hope he's not regretting anything. Davey's come out too, the landlord's son, several teeth short of a sprocket, with his funny pointy head and wingnut ears. His hands sweep incessantly by his sides, fingers splayed wide like bony starfish. Twenty next birth-day on the calendar, a kid of five behind those pale eyes. Still, you don't need many brain cells to climb on a pillion and hold on tight; and it's the rides we've given him Sunday mornings on the trailies up here that's maybe endeared us to his father. Not many, even those with pubs on mountain tops a mile from the nearest house, say yes to bike parties.

The Wraiths have brought kiddies and women and tents with them and they're all smiles and handknit stripey woollies under their leathers. The vans are theirs and we tell them to park them by our old bus round the side of the building. We tuck the bus well out of view from the front because if we don't we never get Davey out of the driver's seat. The Wraiths are West Walian weirdos, into body painting and peace-nik tribalism, but they've ridden the eighty miles east to see us before and everyone likes them. The Dragons are a different breed. We were just wondering, in the minutes before they arrived, whose idea it was to invite them. I said it was Kev's, Kev said no way, it was Pete's, but he denied it too, and in the end we all agreed to blame Dai, who isn't here tonight on account of his girlfriend having their third baby in the Royal Gwent this afternoon. The Dragons are city boys from Swansea. No women or kiddies with them, just six black-leathered blokes on five big black ugly bikes, blokes who stare around the mountain top as if they've never been on one before and are vaguely impressed but are much too hard to be caught saying, 'Ooh, lovely views from up here, boys.' Dunno where they're expecting to sleep; kip where they drop, I suppose.

The hog's been roasting an hour or more now, out in the rear garden. It's a rainthreatening night though and cold for mid-September, so the spit's right by the double doors and screened with tarps against the damp wind. We'll be mostly inside tonight, I reckon. We got to help Tom out behind the bar when he needs it, so I take first stint; there'll be a rush on while the visitors catch up with us. The Wraiths drink real ale, even the women, and the Dragons lager or Newcastle Brown. The last of them are clumping in now. Shit. One of the Dragons is a giant. Seriously. He hits his head on every beam between the front door and the bar. Maybe he thinks he's still wearing his crash hat. He isn't, but being whacked around the head every two seconds doesn't seem to bother him. Must be six foot eight, minimum – he makes Jonno look small, and he's six four.

The landlord stares at him as he approaches and whispers to me out the corner of his mouth, 'Sure I've seen that lad somewhere before', but then shakes his head as if he can't place him. I reckon that at that height you'd see the bloke from practically everywhere. He's not fat but not skinny either. Wonder where he buys his seven-league boots. He's reached the bar now, and his mate is getting him a pint.

'What you having, then, Scum?' the mate asks, and I have a small coughing fit before I can serve them. Scum – shit, who thinks them up? – has lager. Davey is behind the bar with us and is staring at the visitors with his mouth open and his hands flapping. Scum's height is exciting him. In a minute he's going to point. Scum looks as if he doesn't like the attention.

'Don't mind him,' Tom murmurs, flicking a look back at his son. Scum blinks at Tom, and then at me, without altering his expression. His mate says, 'Just a kid, Scum, you heard him,' and leads him away to join their friends at a table.

The band are arriving now, only an hour late. Got lost twice on the way, they say. When they played for us in town last year they didn't get paid, because all the cash had been drunk by the end of the evening, so they're taking precautions tonight by demanding their fifty quid up front. Pete hands it over, plus a dozen pints to get them in the mood, and they start to set up on the stage blocks at the end of the room.

Within half an hour the sounds are making the beams sing, the hog's half demolished, and outside it's pitch, with rain coming down like swords. Every boy returning from the lavs has to shake himself like a dog and you can tell the ones who've only been back a while because there's steam rising off them. The women are luckier – their bogs are inside, although the Dragons have sat themselves by the door, and I've seen both Bethan and Karin have to smack hands on their way in.

The word goes round that the veggie stew – half the

Wraiths are vegetarian – has been spiked with magic mush-rooms. Not sure if this is a joke or a genuine selling ploy. Jonno was certainly wandering the hilltop earlier. Causes a scramble for bowls, whichever. I tell Tom it's a joke, but he says to keep Davey away from the stuff anyway; he's not allowed to drink alcohol, even, because it interferes with his medication.

The bike groups aren't mixing too well. The Wraiths are fine, bopping around to the music with their tiny woolly kids, and the women are chatting to each other, but the Dragons are keeping to themselves. I've finished my bar stint and on our side of the room Jonno is getting edgy. He says the Dragons are after our women, huddled over the tables like that, looking over to us with mean eyes, and Scum's height outrages him. I'm not too worried though; Jonno can see aggression in a dead sheep, undercurrents add spice to a party, and it's not as if the boy can help being tall.

Bethan comes up to me. 'The Wraiths can't put their tents up in this,' she says. 'And the kiddies are tired. I've said they can use the bus, OK?'

'Fine by me.' I glance around to check and everyone nods. There're two double mattresses in the back of the stripped-out bus; enough to sleep the adults too, if they're prepared to bunk up. We can kip in here, if it comes to it.

The kids disappear, the band takes a break, and we're merry enough for the party games to begin. First a cream-cracker eating competition. It's meant to be one from each group taking part, but the Dragons don't seem keen, so it's Kev and Jonno from our lot, and a Wraith called Steve, who's got a smile you could hang washing on and long fair hair to his waist. I see Bethan nudge Karin when he gets up on to the stage and they giggle with their heads together. Lecherous tarts.

The boys are given five cream crackers each, to be eaten

dust dry. Sounds easy, but I've never made it beyond two. The rules say you have to swallow them proper, no holding them in your gob and spraying them out later. They're off.

Shit, Kev appears to have finished his already; he's showing us a disgusting wide-open flaky mouth. No he hasn't, he's stuffed half of them down the split in the back of Jonno's jeans. While Jonno's remonstrating with him – producing a snow blower effect all over the stage, because he's got a mouthful – sneaky Steve munches furiously and finishes his legit. A showman, this boy, gives a big bow to shrieks of approval from the women. His prize is a foot-long bar of chocolate. The women go mad, he's a real honeypot now, greedy slappers. A snog for four squares, he announces, holding it up high as he jumps down from the blocks, and he's practically on the floor by the time they've finished with him.

A few minutes to calm down and refill pints, and it's apple bobbing next. OK, so it's a month early, but who cares. Jonno, still shaking bits of cracker out of the legs of his jeans, carries the brimming steel pail in from the porch, a dozen apples floating on the surface. We had planned to do this outside but I daresay Tom's carpet will recover. Davey is giggling beside me, a high idiot sound, really enjoying this. Hey, a couple of Dragons are going to join in now. Saw what happened to the Wraith, didn't they, fancy winning a mass snog themselves. Two other Wraiths and Pete from our lot line up as well.

'You gotta kneel,' Kev explains. 'Hands behind your back. Anyone's hands come forward, Karin dunks you, got it?'

Karin grins, standing over the pail. Tits quivering under her T-shirt, hands ready. Wouldn't trust her an inch. She once pushed Pete off a small cliff into the sea at Port Eynon, just to make a big splash, she said. Psycho woman.

Pete's going first, trying to nudge the apples to the edge

with his nose to get purchase. Davey is pushing at my shoulder to see better. He looks so eager I ask, 'You want a go, Davey, do you?'

'Nooo.' He finds the idea hysterical. Especially now Karin has lunged downwards and Pete has got a faceful of water. Sure he didn't move his hands. I reckon she just likes him wet.

The two Dragons go next. They're good. Really good. Wonder if they file their teeth. I imagine them practising this on club nights: a really wild bandit skill. Karin nearly dunks the second, but he's too fast for her. He even manages a smile as evil as hers as he looks up at her, the apple still clamped in his mouth.

There's a thump and a curse behind me. Scum's here. He's cracked his head again, stupid sod. But maybe this is his game. Can't damage himself on his knees. His butty – the one who bought him his pint at the bar – shouts from across the room, 'Hands still, Scum,' as he kneels down.

Scum mutters,'Yeah, yeah,' and swings his arms behind his back.

His butty shouts to Karin,'You dunk him, woman, you can get your kit off.'

Scum looks at her – his eyes are on a level with her tits – and says, 'Yeah, kit off.'

'Oi!' Pete protests, as if, Karin being his girl, her protection is down to him. We all have our delusions. No one threatens Karin. Before, Scum'd just have got wet; now he's going to drown.

Davey is jumping up and down beside me. Karin doesn't even wait for Scum to mouth the first apple. She lets him get an inch from the water, then rams his head down into the pail and holds it down. There's a defiant cheer from half the crowd – mostly the women – and a fountain of water and apples sprays over us as Scum struggles free.

Davey pushes past me and jiggles beside Scum, still on his knees, coughing fit to bust.

'Weed in it,' he cries, shrieking with laughter and clutching his groin. He rocks to and fro. 'Ha ha, weed in it.'

'Oh shit,' says Kev beside me, trying not to laugh, 'he's telling us he pissed in the bucket.'

'Ah bollocks,' says Pete, sounding not at all amused, and spits out on to the floor. He's still fairly wet from his dunking. We all believe Davey. The bucket's been waiting outside a while and he's not clever enough to lie.

Scum has stopped coughing. He rises to his feet. He's a head and shoulders taller than Davey and maybe twice the weight. Davey grins up at him, inviting him to share the joke. Davey likes everyone, even ones he's just dropped in the shit. Or the wee. Trouble is, the feeling's not always reciprocated.

Tom has appeared with three mops, which he's thrusting into hands. He pushes between Davey and Scum. 'You touch my boy,' he says, prodding Scum in the chest, 'and you're out of here.' This is more of a threat than it sounds, forty miles east of Swansea, a mile from any kind of cover, and the rain sheeting down. 'Davey,' he says, turning to his son. 'You're a pillock. You tell the man you're sorry.'

Davey puts his hands over his mouth, as if it's got a will of its own and he's trying to stop it laughing, but he doesn't succeed.

Scum's mate has come up. He looks more angry with Karin than Davey.

'You,' he says, pushing his face at Karin. 'What did we say?'

'Dream on, wanker.' Karin flounces her chest at him.

Scum's eyes are locked on Davey. Hard to tell what's going on behind them. Unreadable and near seven-foot tall is dangerous. Kev must sense trouble too, I hear him urging the band members up to their instruments.

'For Chrissake,' says Tom, tensely, 'I'll get rid of the lot of you if you don't wind this down.'

For a moment the atmosphere's deadlocked. Davey is still smiling at Scum, Scum still staring hard back. Then Karin says 'OK,' abruptly. As if she's been thinking, and come to a sudden decision. She taps Scum on the chest to get his attention, says 'You watch me, big boy, never mind him,' grins ferociously, and backs away. She jumps up onto the stage. The guitarist to her left plays a tentative twanging line of *The Stripper*. Karin snaps, 'Shut it,' over her shoulder – instantly obeyed – puts her hands on her hips and leans towards us. 'OK,' she taunts, 'so which of you dicks is joining me?'

That's the way these days. You want a girl to get her kit off, you got to have a bloke doing the same. Not that it's usually a problem; amazing the number of boys who fancy themselves after a skinful – any excuse and they're baring their bits, whether the girls are joining in or not.

This time, though, the decision's made for us. By popular demand. What a surprise, it's Steve the Chocolate Wraith pushed forward. He's not resisting, or even pretending to. Don't suppose it's anything to a Wraith – ride their bikes bollock naked, I dare say, given half a chance and a warmer climate.

He jumps up onto the stage beside Karin, they grind their hips at each other, and the band strike up. Haven't had such a popular pairing for years. They both know what they're doing and once the music and the clapping's going they start to peel off like pros. Top halves first. It's achieving what it's meant to. Scum, who has the best view of all, a foot above everyone else, is transfixed. Quite forgotten young Davey beside him. Davey's pale eyes stare at Karin's chest, wide with wonder. Karin's tits are indeed a wonder, the softest, kindest, most generous part of her. The only boy not watching her is Pete, who sees her tits most nights; he's sulking and rolling himself a cigarette. The women are cheering the Wraith on – he's got Celtic tattoos on his arms, back and pecs, and a nipple ring to match the half-dozen in his ear.

We got a bit of a wait for their lower halves, because the Wraith's wearing boots and they take a while to unlace – elegant-like – and kick off. It all adds to the anticipation. When they finally drop their togs the women are rowdier than the men, lusting and laughing so hard they have to hang on to each other. The men aren't laughing, but not because they aren't appreciating Karin. Women just seem to find naked bodies funnier.

We're all concentrating on the stage show – and not on faces up there either – so it takes a while to twig that Karin and the Wraith aren't looking at us any more, but at something behind us. They glance at each other, grinning wild, and give their moves a whole lot extra punch. Tits and donger whirling around as if they're desperate to meet. Tom's the first to look back and I hear him hiss, 'Stone me, boys, see who's here.' I swing round. There's an old lady behind us. She must have been shaking off her dripping umbrella when she saw what was going on, and she's riveted mid-shake. She's wearing a long fur coat, scarlet lipstick and false eyelashes as big as tarantulas. It's Stella, the lunatic from the nearest house, seventy, she claims, but could pass for ninety. She must know that the pub is closed – she's here every evening – but couldn't resist gatecrashing.

Everyone's spotted her now and the audience is falling about with mirth. The Wraith and Karin stop dancing and stick triumphant thumbs in the air. Show over. Stella says loudly, 'Now don't stop on my account, dearies, I was enjoying that.'

'Sorry Stella,' says Tom, 'but you know you shouldn't be here. Private party, I told you yesterday.'

Stella says, 'Oh they won't mind me, will you dears,' and
settles herself on one of the bar stools. She's walked a mile
to get here, in her fur coat and the lashing rain, so I don't
suppose we will. A few of the Dragons are shaking their
heads with disbelief, but nobody seems hostile. Tom goes
round the counter to get her a rum-and-black.

Pete tries to sell her a raffle ticket.

'What's the prize, dear?' she asks.

'Quart of whisky,' Pete says. 'We'll be drawing soon.'

Stella gets her money out. Her coat has bald patches and
stinks of wet animal. She peers round Pete towards the stage.
'Where's that nice young man with no clothes on?' She
winks the tarantulas at Pete. 'He'd make a pretty prize.'

'Taken already, love,' says Pete, who maybe isn't the best
person to ask about this. 'They're just cutting him up now.'

Stella laughs throatily and hands over a pound coin.

Over at the stage Karin has dressed again and the Wraith
has put his jeans and boots on. He doesn't bother with his
T-shirt – no point having all that torso decoration if you
can't show it off. He bounces over to the bar and Tom sighs,
'You're a braver man than me, boy,' and pulls him a pint on
the house. Pete scowls at him and goes off to reclaim Karin.
Stella asks the Wraith to turn round and hold his hair up so
she can see the designs on his back and when he does she
grabs his flanks and squeezes them, with her mouth oohing
like she's checking ripe fruit. The Wraith laughs and sits
down beside her; watching them you'd think that she was
his cheeky nan and they'd known each other for ever.

Tom is staring around the room as if he's lost something.
'You seen Davey?' he asks me. 'Was here for the dancing,
wasn't he?'

'Certainly was,' I say. 'Didn't miss a second.' But I can't
see him now either. There's a crowd jigging about to the
music and Pete and Karin are snogging in the far corner

but no sign of that pointy head anywhere. Maybe he found Karin's dancing so exciting he's gone somewhere quiet to dwell on it.

'I'll just check upstairs,' Tom says, as if the same thought's occurred to him, and asks me to watch the bar. But before I've served a couple of pints he comes back frowning and says he can't find him. He stares round the room again.

'That tall boy's not here either,' he says. 'You seen him?'

He sounds a mite anxious. Not like Tom; he's not the father-hen type. But we're both remembering the way Scum was looking at Davey before Karin distracted him.

'I'll check the bogs,' I say. I could do with a slash anyway.

It's still sheeting down outside and there's no one in the outhouse except a squadron of moths taking turns to dive-bomb the light bulb. Returning to the bar I bump into Scum's mate.

'Hey,' I say. Don't want to put anyone's hackles up, but a quiet word shouldn't hurt. 'We lost the landlord's son. The funny kid.' I flap my hands by my waist to jog his memory. 'And your friend Scum's missing too. Tom's worrying.'

The man's swaying. He's pissed but his brain's still functioning. He turns to scan the crowd.

'Tom's checked upstairs,' I say. 'And there's no one in the bogs.'

'Ah fuck it.' The bloke thumps the arm of the Dragon next to him. 'Oi. Looks like Scum and that kid have gone AWOL. Better go out and check.'

The Dragon stares at him – everyone's taking a moment to react on account of the alcohol – then says, 'Rhys has got a torch. Hey Rhys,' he calls across the table, 'give us your torch. Jay's lost Scum out there. May be with that dribbler kid.'

Rhys says, 'Shit,' and tosses a rubber torch across. Jay and his friend leave. I decide to get a torch off Tom. On my way to the bar Rhys intercepts me. 'Any of your boys out there looking?'

'Not yet,' I say. 'Just getting a torch off the landlord.'

Rhys hesitates, as if deciding how much to confide, and then says, 'You want to go easy on Scum if you find him. Looks OK but there's nothing up there.' He touches his temple. 'Let Jay handle him. Scum listens to Jay.'

Tom has come up, already holding a torch, and has overheard Rhys. Something seems to click in his brain.

'Knew I'd seen him before. Bugger me. Simple, isn't he? Took Davey on a horse-riding weekend over Llandovery way. Four, five years ago. That boy was one of the older kids.' He holds his hand an inch above his head. 'Only so high then, mind.'

I think back to Davey's excitement on first seeing Scum, and his delight at watching him get dunked.

'I think Davey recognized him,' I say. 'Yeah, I'm sure he did.' Not that I know what to make of this. Does it make the situation less or more dicey?

'That lad doesn't ride a bike now, does he?' Tom sounds astonished.

'Course not,' scoffs Rhys. 'Goes two up with Jay. Jay's his brother. Do anything for Scum, Jay would. Takes him everywhere.'

'Christ though, I remember, he had a temper.' Tom frowns again. He clicks the torch on. 'There's another in the porch.' He nods at me. 'You coming?'

He finds me the torch, tucked up in the porch rafters, and we step outside. Neither of us are wearing jackets and my T-shirt's drenched in seconds. The rain's like white rods in the torch beam.

The hillside round the front of the Talywain is old hummocky workings, split by the long access track. Tom shouts for Davey a couple of times and when there's no reply he says he's going round the back to the paddock and sheds. I say I'll stay here and check the hummocks out. I run up the sides and shine the torch down into the hollows. Get a fright on the second, seeing a heap at the bottom, but turns out to be a pile of sodden tarps left over from screening the spit. I'm trying to think straight through the beer and half the time I'm thinking that the two boys will turn up safe somewhere we haven't thought of and this is a panic for nothing, and the rest of the time I'm imagining Davey smashed to a pulp in the mud by someone who doesn't know when to stop, and my heart's thundering and I know Tom's going to say that this is all our fucking fault.

There's lights ahead, further down the track. A torch light and the headlight of a bike. I make my way towards them. It's the two Dragons. Jay still has the torch and his friend is wheeling his bike, swinging the front from side to side to illuminate the banks and ditches.

Jay is in a spitting temper. 'Fucking rain,' he swears, 'could have gone over a fucking cliff in this. That fucking stupid kid.'

I tell him there aren't any quarry cliffs round here and he whips round as if I'm picking an argument and he wants to hit me. I know it's worry making him angry but it doesn't stop my temper rising too. Bloody Dragons. Trouble wherever they go.

'It's your brother that's causing the problem,' I snap. 'He's why we're out here drowning. Davey's not going to thump anyone.'

'Who says Scum is?' he shouts back. 'Just cos he's slow doesn't mean he's a maniac.'

As we're walking we kind of bump shoulders with each other. Partly because of the dark and the uneven track, partly because we're pissed and getting irritable. When we bump a second time Jay suddenly seems to snap. He hisses, 'Fuck

off, bastard,' and gives me a big push, sending me sliding
into the ditch at the side.

Bastard yourself, I think, picking myself out of the mud.
I'm outraged – what the hell does he think I'm doing out
here? Getting drenched and freezing and missing the fun
inside. And this is the thanks I get. Sod his brother. I'm going
to clout him one he'll remember.

Jay knows I'm coming back for him and plants his feet
steady. It'll only be one to one, because his friend's holding
the bike and won't let that drop in a hurry.

I'm just aiming a fist at him when we hear a cry. A kiddie's
cry. It's like someone slapped the both of us. A yell loud
enough to be heard over the rain.

I say, 'Shit, that's a Wraith kid, they're in the bus,' and stare
at Jay. He stares back. Then we start running.

I know the way in the dark better than Jay, so I'm in front
as we get round the side of the pub. It's lighter here because
there's a lamp left on for the kids. I can see Tom, tugging at
the driver's door of the bus, and there's a little kid standing
at the open rear door, facing us, screaming his head off.

He stops when he sees us, seems to think a moment, and
then shouts at us, 'We wanna go. Tell 'em it's our turn. 'Tis'n
fair. 'Tis'n fair.'

I suddenly guess what's going on, and feel the adrenalin
drain away. The bus, Davey's favourite toy, it's obvious.
Well, obvious if you see the boys' vanishing act as Davey's
idea, not Scum's. It's all kids together out here, but the big-
gest ones are hogging the fun. I slow down and walk up to
Tom. He's just got the door open, because there aren't any
locks and he's stronger than Davey, and Davey's hanging on
to the steering wheel like a limpet and wailing at him. Scum
is sitting in the front passenger seat holding an imaginary
wheel and making farting tractor noises. Another Wraith kid
is behind Scum, banging him around the head with his tiny

fists, which Scum's ignoring, and a third child is squeezed between the seats, flicking dash switches on and off and saying, 'Systems on, ready for take-off, brrumm ... eeeow ... ' to no one in particular. The handbrake's off, but the bus is on level mud and doesn't look like it's moved. I thank the shit Jonno didn't leave the keys in here.

Jay gets Scum out his door and Tom eventually manages to prise Davey's hands off the wheel and pull him out too. I tug the handbrake tight on again and tell the kids I'm getting their mums here to sort them out. Though this doesn't seem to scare them – they're shouting, 'Bye bye ha ha ha,' at Scum and Davey as we lead the boys away.

In the porch Tom reads the riot act to Davey and Jay does the same to Scum. They're a lot drier than the rest of us; we look like shipwreck survivors. And I'm pasted with mud, too. Jay grins at me, loosened up now he knows Scum's safe, and says, 'Hey, sorry butt, freaked a bit out there,' and I nod at him and say, 'A pint'll wash it off, ta.'

We've only been gone from the party a few minutes, though it feels longer. We squelch in and find everything much as we left it: the band still playing, a crowd dancing, Pete and Karin still snogging each other senseless in the corner. Stella's at the bar still downing rum-and-blacks, and Steve the Chocolate Wraith is still half naked beside her; except, blow me, some bastards have it lucky; now there's a quart of fucking whisky on the bar counter in front of him.

# SEDUCING HIM

Yes, yes, this is right. This nakedness, this straining flesh.
He and I, come full circle …

… And I'm coping. He's here, and we're getting somewhere.
He arrived just an hour ago, as they wheeled me into the
delivery room. I was having a contraction, and I bawled at
him. Only with relief; I was so scared he wouldn't come.
These last weeks he's blown wild and tame. Didn't see him
at all over the weekend. Out both nights, his sister says, not
home till morning, stinking of beer. But then round to me
Monday evening, irresistible on the doorstep, smiling his
easy, blue-eyed smile. Pressed his hands against my lump
– our lump, his fierce hands said – and kissed me, hard, on
the lips.
  But he's made no commitment; whim brought him here
today.
  The nurses are like cheerleaders. 'Push, push,' they cry …

… God. But better that time. Less in my throat.
  A strange calm, this in-between time. The whole room
pulls back, waiting for me. I feel myself regather.

I remember telling him I was pregnant. Outside his work, in the street, a blurted, throw-away line. How did I do it? He was a stranger. He was. I knew his body, God, his sweet body, but he, he was a stranger.

I look back at myself, and marvel. So besotted, but so brave too, so determined.

Here it comes. In my chest first, the edge of a relentless weight …

… Oh, the power of if it. If this force were harnessed, if we could summon it at will …

He never doubted the baby was his. Some men would have. Some men would have said it, even if they hadn't believed it, just to stab their way out. He was stunned. He was dismayed. Yes, at first he was. But he believed me. And accepted it. I'll always love him for that.

And look at him now … ah, his expression. Who else can have seen that? Such naked tenderness. Not his mates. Not his old girlfriends. Not me, till now. I want to crush it to my breast, imprint it on my heart. Yes, such power. I'm his mother, father, lover, creator …

I remember his power, and how it swept me away. Is this how he felt, nine months ago, when he seduced me? …

… They're telling me not to push, next time. It's close, it's close. The nurses are brisker, sharper-tongued. I'm a process, suddenly, not a person. He's sensed it, he's standing up, peering across me. I need his hand … oh, Christ …

… It didn't come that time. Let it be soon. The violence of it. I hate panting. It's like fighting myself.

At the antenatal class I was the only one without a man. Ask him, the teacher urged, you never know. I will, I promised, but I lied. I couldn't risk it.

And he's confused now. His ignorance is frightening him. He's asking the midwife if something's wrong. He says I'm exhausted. Am I exhausted? I've never felt this way before, I don't know. It's beyond exhaustion. Beyond everything. The midwife's smiling. Relax Dad, she says, she's doing fine. Dad. He's shocked. Oh, his face. It's suddenly occurred to him that I am Mum, and he is Dad. That this is how it is. I want to laugh at him, at his astonishment. He never realized ...

... Not that time, either. Oh God. Oh God. I'm a drumtight fruit, about to split apart. Something fleshy, juicy, exotic. Mango, kumquat, pomegranate, pawpaw, passion fruit. Will it hurt? It must hurt. Such soft flesh, such a merciless force.

His face is tense and still. So beautiful. My beautiful, untamed, helpless man. I feel spectacular. Spectacularly ugly, spectacularly beautiful. I am huge, all-encompassing, omnipotent. I am the centre of the universe.

Here it comes. Oh God ...

... She is on my belly. My child. Our child. Blood and mucus and warm stickiness. My flesh is white, flaccid, spent. Hers, mottled pink, plump and alive. Where we touch the substance of me seems to enfold her. I am adrift, way up here, but my body is earthbound, motherbound, and knows what to do.

I am pure animal, and the world is singing.

He is bending over us, recalling me. His hand smooths

damp strands of hair off my forehead. His touch is dry and cool. Now his lips brush my naked shoulder.

The nurses have cut the cord; our daughter is squirming across my breasts. There, she has found a nipple; such eager jaws, clamping and chewing.

His fingertips circle, oh so reverently, the damp crown of her head. His expression is soft and foolish.

He lifts his gaze to me, and I see surrender. I can walk inside now, claim what I like.

# OF SONS AND STARS

'This can't take long,' said Susan, pulling the heavy latched door of the cottage to behind her. 'I've got to ring your father before ten.'

'Just along here,' said Jamie's voice, disembodied in the darkness, somewhere the other side of the garden lawn. 'It has to be away from the lights.'

Susan sighed, and with an edge of humour she didn't actually feel, said, 'This had better be worth it.' She stepped, reluctantly, onto the dewy grass. Her canvas shoes were going to get soaked. Where was her son taking her? Ugh, she could feel a chilly dampness already. At the bottom of the lawn she heard a familiar rattle and creak. Oh God, he was through into the field. Groping for the swinging garden gate she called irritably, 'Where are we going, Jamie?' Then made an effort – this was meant to be a surprise for her, a treat, even – and called again, more lightly,'Jamie?'

'Here.' There was still eagerness in her son's voice. She felt a pang of shame, and then gratitude, for the uncrushable optimism and tolerance of her child. She sighed again. Why were his surprises so wearisome? Why did they oppress her so? And what would it be, this time? Probably an animal. That's why he wouldn't use the handlamp. A hedgehog?

Toad? Glow-worm? Something of wonder to a thirteen-year-old. She could hear herself saying, fervently, 'Oh, marvellous, Jamie.' Feeling dutiful, for expressing wonder, and inadequate, for having to pretend it.

In the darkness she stumbled over a tussock of long scratchy grass. 'Oh hell,' she said, forgetting good intentions and thinking of her tights, 'Jamie! Put the bloody torch on.'

'You don't need it,' said Jamie's voice, close beside her. 'This'll do. Stand still.'

Susan stood still. The lights of the house had disappeared behind the garden hedge. She could only just make out Jamie, a darker, denser shape in the blackness.

'Well?' she said.

'Look up.'

She looked up vaguely. 'What?'

'Oh Mummy.' Jamie sounded exasperated. 'Look.'

She stared up and felt, as a telescopic process, her vision stretch outwards into the night. Her eyes refocused. Millions of stars, from brilliant cats'-eyes to diamond dust, arched in a frozen swirl across the night sky.

'It's the Milky Way,' she said. Of course, she had seen it before, often. But still. Sincerely she said, 'Beautiful, isn't it.' Her son had brought her out to see the stars. How touching. She wondered how long she should stay, marvelling at them, to show her appreciation.

'Now,' Jamie said, sounding not awestruck, but business-like. 'Come closer.'

Oh dear, there was more. Susan twisted her wrist, before realizing she wouldn't be able to read her watch. Suppressing a tick of impatience – it must be nearly ten – she moved closer.

'Right,' Jamie said. He was so near she could hear the catarrhal rasp of his breathing. He's as tall as I am, she thought. He seems even taller in the dark. But he still breathes like a child. His elbow brushed against her arm, as he did something with the torch.

'OK,' he said. 'Now, get really close, and follow the line of the beam. Keep behind it, or you'll be dazzled.'

She heard a click. From his chest a powerful beam shot upwards to the sky.

'Gracious!' she said. For a second the beam looked like a heart-light, emerging from her son, leading straight up to the stars. She recollected herself, and gave a short laugh. 'You must have bought a new battery.'

'Yup,' said Jamie, sounding smug. 'You need a powerful torch for this.'

He swung the beam from horizon to horizon like a search-light, then steadied it.

'Put your head close to mine.' He waited for Susan to obey him. 'Right, now, that group of stars there. Can you see them?'

Susan followed the line of the beam upwards. How impressive. She could see exactly the stars he meant, just outside the dense swirl of the Milky Way. The beam appeared to bathe them in pale light. She nodded and said, 'Yes, I see them.'

'That's Orion.'

'Is it?' she said. 'How clever of you. And what a good way of pointing them out. It's like using a ruler on a blackboard.' She pulled back. 'Where on earth did you learn to do this?'

'On the geography field trip,' Jamie said. 'Mr Haines is mad about stars.' He moved the beam a fraction away. 'There, that's the Pleiades ... see? And that bright star there ... Aldebaran. In Taurus.'

'Where's ... um ...' It took Susan a second to think of a heavenly body, ' ... the Plough?'

'Ah,' said Jamie. 'That's the other side of the Milky Way.' He swung the beam across the sky and resettled it. 'There ... see?'

'Goodness,' breathed Susan. 'This really is clever.'

'It is, isn't it?' Jamie sounded pleased. 'And look, there's the Bear. There ... there ... and there.'

Susan looked at the stars that made up the Bear. He'd learnt this on his geography field trip. She frowned. 'But the school trip ...' she said. 'It was ages ago.' Her son must have known how to do this for months.

'Yeah, well, it's a good night, tonight,' said Jamie. 'You can't always see so much, can you?'

It occurred to her, shockingly, that her son must know other things he hadn't told her about. That he was no longer totally known to her. And he must have been out here, surely, practising this...

'I'll show you something else, too, if you like,' said Jamie. 'Nothing to do with astronomy ... about your eyes.'

'What?' She glanced back from the sky to the faint outline of his upturned face. For a moment it looked unfamiliar. Stronger-featured, solider. Almost adult.

'Well,' he said, adjusting the direction of the torch beam. 'Look at that empty space ... there ... a sort of triangle ... look straight at it.'

Susan lifted her eyes back up to the sky. 'I'm looking.'

Jamie clicked the torch off. 'Now move your eyes somewhere else, but remember where the space is.'

'What d'you mean?'

'Just do it. Don't move your eyes too far. Remember where the space is, relative to where you're looking.'

'OK,' said Susan slowly. 'I've done it.'

'Now,' said Jamie. 'Don't look back, but what's in the space now?'

Susan concentrated on seeing the space, without actually looking at it. The sky, on that side of the vision, now appeared crowded with stars. 'I can't find it,' she said. 'It's gone. Sorry.'

'Look back to where it was,' said Jamie.

Susan looked back. The black triangle was instantly visible. How could she have missed it?

'I've got it,' she said. 'I don't know why I couldn't see it before.'

'Because it wasn't there,' said Jamie triumphantly.

'What are you talking about?' Susan smiled. 'Obviously it was there.'

'It wasn't,' said Jamie. 'Try moving your eyes away again.'

Susan stared at the space, fixing it, and then gradually moved her eyes away. As she did, the space appeared to fill with tiny dimlit stars. She looked back, and it was a space again.

'My God,' she said. 'Stars appeared in the hole.'

Jamie chuckled. 'Brilliant, isn't it?'

'But how can stars suddenly appear like that? Are they real? Why can't I see them when I look at them?'

'Oh, they're real all right,' said Jamie. 'It's because of the angle light hits the back of our eyes.' He switched the hand-lamp on and pointed it down at the grass by their feet. 'See the bright inner circle ... how small it is, straight down? Now ...' He raised the lamp slightly, so the beam hit the grass obliquely, about six foot away. 'See how much bigger it is now ... how much more grass it's covering? That's why our peripheral vision is so good. Light coming in at an angle hits more cones in our eyes. So we can see things that are too faint to see straight on.'

Susan stared at the oblong of light on the field, then raised her eyes to the sky. She found the empty black triangle. Very slowly she shifted her eyes away. Once more the dimlit stars appeared. Extraordinary.

She thought a moment and then said, 'Is this always true? When we look at things straight on, we never see them as clearly as when we don't?'

She sensed Jamie shrug. 'I suppose so. As long as they're in our field of vision. It's just how the eye works.'

'Did Mr Haines teach you this, too?'

'Mmm ... sometimes we couldn't see all the right stars in a constellation. You move your eyes away, and then you can.'

'It's amazing,' said Susan. She felt truly amazed, at learning something so fundamental, for the first time. And amazed too, in some all–encompassing, revelatory way, at her son.

Jamie turned the beam of the torch upwards, under-lighting his face. He said 'Hoo hoo,' and grinned at her ghoulishly.

She grinned back at him. Immediately he was just Jamie again, her son, ordinary, unamazing Jamie.

She looked away, back up to the stars, and reassuringly, out of the corner of her eye, saw her son grow amazing again. She felt suddenly light, almost giddy. As if a burden – a burden she had scarcely realized she was carrying – had lifted from her. It was floating upwards: the weight of a child – her child – drifting up to the stars. She watched it rise, dwindling to nothingness in the vast night sky. There, it was gone.

She turned back to Jamie with a smile. Her tall, nearly adult, unwearisome son. And recalled, seeing him, that she had a phone call to make.

'I've got to go in,' she said. She touched his sleeve. 'I must ring your father.'

Jamie said, 'Oh yeah,' with sudden enthusiasm, and bounded towards the garden gate. He swung the beam of the torch behind him, lighting her path. 'I'll tell him about showing you the stars, shall I?'

'Definitely,' she said, and followed him towards the house.

# ANOTHER SUDDEN DEATH

As I enter the interview room I nod across to Pascoe, the duty social worker.

'Charles,' I say. We're on first name terms.

He nods back. 'Mike.'

The boy at the table looks up at me with dry, fierce eyes.

I make myself comfortable the other side of the table. There's no hurry, it's a quiet night. I unfold a sheet of paper the collator's just given me and study it. He's written the boy's name, Paul, at the top, and underneath listed eight addresses. Dates beside them, all within the last two months. One a week, looks like.

I switch on the tape, make the introductions, and then read out the top four addresses. 'Numbers 12, 20, 42 and 56 Rosebury Avenue.' I glance up. The boy's got long lank blue-black hair – dyed, almost certainly – and sharp, sallow features. The hint of lines, already, round his mouth and eyes. He's fifteen. Fifteen, going on thirty-five.

I read on down the list. 'Aylesham Avenue, numbers 12, 36 and 50. And number 70 tonight. Busy lad, eh?'

The boy flicks hooded eyes back at Pascoe. It looks an insolent gesture but I know these lads. And he's sweating; a strand of black gipsy hair is glued across his right cheekbone. Shit scared; first collar, and only fifteen.

I speak across to Pascoe. Some lads find it easier to inter-
rupt than answer direct. 'Creature of habit, this one.' I don't
have to pretend to sound weary. 'Rosebury and Aylesham.
Within a spit of each other, both off Commercial Road. All
corner properties ...'

A muscle has twitched in the boy's face. Aha ... it comes
as a shock to them, that someone's been analyzing their
crimes.

Pascoe returns my gaze stolidly. His powerful body is
relaxed, arms folded across his barrel chest. He sports a
grizzled, sea-captain beard. Mr Neutral. I continue.

'And all on south sides of the roads.' I'm going to push.
'We know it's this lad, see. Because of the photos.'

That stirs Pascoe. 'You've got photos?' His beard juts out at
the boy almost belligerently.

'Oh, not us. Him. It's what he does. His trademark. Gets
his scissors out. Hacks up photographs.'

Pascoe's expression says he didn't know this. I let the nas-
tiness of it curl in the air. The boy has tucked his chin into
his chest and is studying his lap.

I lean forward. 'What you got against pictures, lad?'

'Fuck off.' The boy speaks in a harsh whisper, without lifting his head.

Well. At least he's talking. Maybe we're in business. I tap
the sheet of paper.

'These addresses. All yours, aren't they?'

The boy lifts his head and swallows, his adam's apple
leaping. His neck belongs to a frightened kid, but his voice,
when it comes, is still harsh.

'You don't know that.'

I sigh. 'Well, it was you this evening, wasn't it? At number
70. Think there are two of you? Two hoodlums rifling
through drawers, bookcases, cupboards. Cutting up snaps.
Of families, children, girlfriends ...'

'Might be,' the boy mutters.

'And I might be your grandmother.'

The boy lurches towards me. 'You don't know,' he hisses. 'You don't fucking know.'

'Paul,' says Pascoe warningly. 'Easy now.'

'OK,' I say. 'OK son.' The boy's near the edge. I watch the tension in his body subside. Anger and fear. Careful with this one.

The boy slumps back in his chair. Two livid spots have appeared on his cheekbones. His eyes are still brilliant with anger.

I'm about to speak again when the door opens. The smooth, pale-skinned face of DI Johnson appears.

'Can I have a word?' His yellow-brown eyes pass over Pascoe and settle on the boy.

'Right now?' I ask, reaching for the tape machine. Dammit.

Johnson's staring at the boy. 'If you wouldn't mind.' The boy returns his gaze glitteringly.

I suspend the interview and scrape my chair back. 'Won't be a minute.'

Out in the corridor Johnson apologizes; CID need to borrow two uniformed officers. 'OK,' I say, suppressing impatience. At least Johnson had the courtesy to ask. 'You can have Price and Datta.'

I'm reaching back for the door handle when Johnson asks, 'Who's the boy?'

'Our scissor-happy burglar. Screwball. Been working his way through Rosebury and Aylesham.'

Johnson looks thoughtful. 'Got form, has he?'

Does Johnson know something? 'No record,' I say, cautiously.

'Funny.' Johnson strokes a finger over his lips. 'Sure I know him.' He squints into the distance. 'That face ... I've seen it somewhere.'

I recall the way the boy met his gaze. 'He doesn't seem to know you.'

'No,' Johnson nods, conceding it.

I hesitate. If Johnson says he knows a face, he most likely knows it. He's a genius, visually. Got an eye for structure: noses, lips, eyes, features that don't change. And a picture-book memory that goes back years.

Johnson is making chewing movements with his jaw, as if he's tasting the image of the boy. All his pictures have a flavour: good, bad, hot, cold.

'Well?' I ask.

'Not good,' he says, and pulls a face.

I mustn't miss anything. 'I'll bear it in mind,' I say.

I don't return to the interview room immediately, but nip back down the corridor to the collator.

Jim is sticking coloured tape onto his eight-foot wall chart. This means he's not busy.

'Jim?' I say. 'I'm still interviewing my burglar boy. There's a whiff of something here. Can you try again? By place this time? Rosebury and Aylesham Avenue.'

Jim detaches a dangling roll of red sticky tape from his teeth. 'What, scene of crime? Home addresses?'

'Either. Anything. Probably nothing. But just look, will you?'

He snorts. I raise my thumb. He's a good lad, Jim.

Now back to the interview room. Well well. Pascoe's been trying his luck. His chair's pulled up close to the boy's and he's leaning forward, an elbow on one knee. The boy's hunched in his seat, looking boxed-in. Pascoe doesn't pussy-foot, gives it to them straight. I restart the tape.

'I've explained considerations,' Pascoe says matter-of-factly. 'He agrees all the addresses.'

The boy straightens and attempts a look of triumph. 'I don't have to say no more.' He checks with Pascoe. 'That's right, isn't it?'

Pascoe's done it all. I'm tempted. Eight clear-ups in one short evening. Charge the boy, and move on.

Except for the boy's face, where it shouldn't be, in Johnson's head.

I sit down, to slow the pace. Think a moment.

Then ask, 'Why d'you cut up photos?'

The boy's eyes refer me to Pascoe. 'He says he doesn't like them,' Pascoe says. His tone implies that I'm off territory.

Irritation makes me pursue it. Enough times we're criticized for not looking beyond the crime. 'Really?' I say. I'm ignoring Pascoe, speaking to the boy. 'And why don't you like them?'

The boy's body tightens. 'Just don't.'

'Why?' I repeat.

The boy's tense as a cat now. He shakes his head. 'Don't have to say.'

'If you don't like photographs,' I persist, 'why d'you go looking for them?'

The boy makes a guttural noise in his throat. The hair at the back of my neck rises. I've been here before. Pulled on a casual rope and found something, down in the murk. Do I want to get it up? Is it nasty enough – criminally nasty enough – to be our business? Or should we leave it for Pascoe to haul in, if he can?

The boy's face is grey, his shoulders are swaying.

'Get him some water,' Pascoe says. He's angry.

Eight break-ins in two roads. All near-identical properties. All south-siders. All on corners. More than a whiff here. But I need time.

'I'll do better,' I say, rising. 'I'll get some tea.'

I arrange it with the desk constable on my way upstairs to CID. Hope Johnson's still here. He's got the end window desk in the open-plan office, overlooking the station entrance. He's here, leaning back in his chair, an unopened file on his desk, fingers locked behind his head. His eyes are closed.

I stare down at him. Can't help a smile. 'Any thoughts?'

Johnson's eyes open. The pale irises seem to shrink and darken as he locates himself. Then he says, 'He's older.'

'What, since you saw him?'

Johnson hesitates. 'Maybe I'm wrong … it's recent, the picture I've got … but he's younger. The same, but younger. I think he's fairer, too.'

'He's only fifteen,' I say. 'They change fast.'

Johnson looks unconvinced.

'I'm getting Jim to run through Rosebury Avenue and Aylesham, see if he comes up with anything.'

Johnson picks at the edge of the unopened file on his desk. 'Another thing,' he says slowly. 'If the boy wasn't downstairs, alive and kicking, I'd have said he was dead.'

I feel that prickling again, down my spine. I give a short laugh. 'He's not a ghost, I promise.'

'No.' Johnson is frowning down at the file. 'But that's where I see him. With the dead kids.'

I can't hold faces like Johnson can, but even I've got a few of those. Only a few, mercifully: faces you definitely don't need. Faces, like ghosts, that haunt you.

'Probably the wrong kid,' I say quietly.

'Maybe,' says Johnson.


Back in the collator's office Jim hands me two cards.

'That's all I got. Unless you want to go way back.'

The first is a Mrs Sharples. Number 5 Rosebury Avenue. Three arrests in the past year. Shoplifting.

'Map?' I say.

Jim's got the street map ready. 'There.' He points. The north side of the road. Not on a corner. Unpromising.

I look at the other card. Number 70. Christ. Seventy,

that's where the boy was picked up tonight. I scan the card. Sudden death. Five, no, six months ago. Alan Roberts. Single. Age, fifty-two. No action taken. Natural causes. Hell.

'Why've we got this here?' It rings no bells. Middle-aged man drops dead in his own house, unsuspiciously. 'Why's this on file?'

'Search me.' Jim peers over my shoulder. He points to the reference name at the bottom. 'Ask Johnson.'

On the stairs back up to CID I'm waylaid by a breathless constable. 'Pascoe's getting stroppy,' he says. 'Wants to know when you're going to charge the boy.'

'Soon,' I say, brushing past. 'Tell him soon.'

I slam the card down in front of Johnson.

'That's where we picked up the boy tonight.'

Johnson traces a finger across the card. 'What was he nicking?'

'Not a lot. Some cash. Mostly he was cutting up photographs.'

Johnson says, 'Photographs?' and then in a hollow voice, 'Christ.'

'Mean something to you?'

Johnson gets up. 'Photos. You should have said. I'll get the file.'

He leaves the room. I tear the top sheet off his telephone pad in case I need to take notes. Johnson's a doodler. The page is cluttered with flower sketches, intricately detailed, like botanical drawings. Irises, roses, daffodils. The man's an eccentric.

He returns carrying a marbled grey box file. He puts it on the desk and flips it open. Inside there's a jumble of papers. He picks out two manila envelopes, A4 size. Each has a white address label, handwritten in backward sloping script. 'Tony?' asks Johnson. 'Or Paul?'

'Paul,' I say. I'm getting a bad feeling about this.

Johnson loosens the flap of the envelope and slides the contents onto the desk. A glossy wodge of black and white photographs. Loose strips of negatives. 'Just luck we found them,' he says. 'We were looking for his address book. Dirty bugger.'

I stare down at the top photograph. Stupidly, I see a fish. A long white cold fish, stiff and dead, on a pebble beach. Then the pebble beach becomes a mottled carpet. The fish, a naked child.

'Is that our boy?' I ask. It's difficult to tell. The fish child is fair. With the tip of a finger I push the image aside. In the next photo the boy is on his back, half risen, his torso supported on his elbows. An awkward, unnatural pose. Someone has told him to hold it, right there.

'That's him,' says Johnson. 'Couple of years ago, maybe. Christ. Look at his eyes.'

They're staring straight up at us. It's our boy. In shock, or drunk maybe, or drugged. But definitely our boy. The eyes of a dying child. I wrench my own away. I've seen enough. 'What about Tony?'

'Tony's younger. Nine-ish. In most he's crying.'

'Bastard.'


When we've decided what to do we have Pascoe up. Johnson's taking over – he's got the authority. So it's between him and Pascoe, and Pascoe has no objections once he hears Johnson out, though he reminds us that if we go through with it we won't be able to charge the boy. That's OK. It's a first offence. A caution'll do.

On the way back to the interview room I pick up a metal waste-paper bin. Johnson dismisses the constable on the door, and Pascoe moves his chair to the far wall, so he's not overlooking the boy.

Johnson tells the boy we've got his photographs, and how we got them. He speaks slowly and says everything at least twice, especially about the man being dead.

'You understand?' he says.

Since Johnson started talking the boy's eyes have been locked on his face, as if it's the only safe place to be. The rest of us don't exist. Several times, as if it's a nervy mannerism, he tucks his hair behind his ears. Hair that now, a couple of years on, he chooses to dye black. He jerks his head.

'Was anyone else involved, Paul?' Johnson asks. 'Either before, or when the photos were taken?' Crucial, this; we stop now, if there was.

The boy shakes his head. I believe him. He's too fazed to lie.

Before he hands the photos and negatives over Johnson checks a last time with me. It's destruction of evidence. But the man's dead, and the boy's innocent. He didn't know the house, wasn't even sure of the road. Didn't know the man was dead. Just needed his pictures. Maybe we'll see him again, maybe we won't. He deserves one chance.

Johnson hands over the brown envelope. My respect for him soars; I don't think I could have done it. The boy'll have to check the photos, to be sure. Even Pascoe looks tense. I give the boy the bin, and a box of matches.

Then Johnson and I leave the room.

We'll caution him later. It's Pascoe's business now.

# MUSTARD

Where d'you get mustard, seven o'clock Friday evening, in the back-of-beyond Welsh countryside? Hell and blast. The village shop is closed. When isn't it. The yob at the garage is apologetic. Got petrol, sir, he says, but no mustard. A comedian. Mrs Crabb by the chapel, who cleans the cottage, has got mustard, but won't give me any. Just picked up her half-squeezed tube of it and simpered, 'Well, I can't really give you any of this, Mr T, can I?' Yes you could, you cretinous woman, I thought, you could squeeze some into an egg-cup and give it to me. But I didn't say it, because her idiocy paralyzed me, and I can't go back there now. Shame Mrs Crabb isn't Welsh, bet any of the other villagers would have offered me the whole tube. And then bellyached about it afterwards, but who cares. I'd have got it.

So why do I need mustard, seven o'clock Friday evening? Well, I need it to go with that enormous steak, a good pound-weighter, that's sitting, dripping deliciously, in the kitchen fridge. The steak I bought this afternoon, in a small town somewhere off the M4 where nobody knows me, and which I have to eat, and destroy the evidence of eating, before eleven tonight. That's when Miranda's taxi will arrive from the station, after her working dinner in Bristol. And I cannot eat it, I will not eat it, without mustard. The crime must be perfect.

I suppose I could try the Little Chef, back down on the main road. Order a coffee, and nick some of their mustard sachets by the till. Or do they have those obscene squidgy yellow tomatoes on the tables? Would one of those fit in a pocket? Anyway, it's a forty minute round trip. Oh Christ.

It seems extraordinary that we don't have mustard here, in the cottage store cupboard. But I've just checked again, and we don't. God knows, we use enough at home, to flavour all those disgusting lentil soups.

The stupid cow wears leather, of course. Ho ho. She eats cheese, drinks milk, wears leather. 'How d'you think they produce milk?' I've asked her. 'What d'you suggest they do with all the little baby boy calves the cows have to give birth to, so you can have your precious milk and cheese? Sell them as pets? Return them to the wild?'

Miranda becomes sulky when she's forced to rationalize her vegetarianism. She's too lazy to go the whole hog – my, I am witty tonight – and become a vegan, and anyway she thinks it's cranky. Sandals and beads and back-to-the-earth New Ageism; not her scene at all. And all her women friends are vegetarian, it's practically *de rigeur* these days.

I should have stood up for myself years ago. Men need meat. It's lack of meat that makes us wimps. Welshmen eat meat. Look at all the bloody sheep. They're not ashamed of rearing meat. What else could they farm on all these sodding mountains? Something pretty, for people like Miranda? Tulips, maybe? Shifty-faced Tucker now, at the bottom of the lane, he gets meat every day. Thinks we're mad. Meat every day, roast beef on Sunday, all on less than 200 quid a week. And look at us: 50 thou a year between us, no kids, a flat in London and a cottage in Wales, and we live on lentils and beans. How times change.

Why should I care whether Miranda knows about the steak? Hell, I'm not frightened of her. But it's the subversiveness that appeals. I shall enjoy it more, marinated in deceit. Oh, I shall. But I must have mustard.

Tucker. He'd have it. That roast beef. And he owes us. All those cheeses we gave his dopey wife a fortnight ago, after we'd had the Simpsons down – a dollop of mustard'd be the least we deserve. Dolcelatte, Cambozola, a great wedge of that god-awful Gruyère. Miranda took them down to the farmhouse in a basket, lady bountiful in green wellingtons, picking her way through the mud and muck and his pack of belly-crawling sheepdogs. Pressed them on Mrs Tucker. 'Oh, but we absolutely insist, I'm sure the village shop doesn't run to Dolcelatte, such a shame to think of food wasted.' We could have taken them back to London with us. But no, Miranda says, they'll stink the car out. Liar. She was just struck on impressing the natives.

I'll go down there now. And this time take an egg-cup. Be prepared.

Christ, that's better. I say it myself, I'm a mean chef. A pound of rare steak. Black pepper and mustard. Mangetout and cucumber salad. Three – just three – new potatoes. Two glasses of Burgundy. Ah, Burgundy. What's the point of red wine without red meat? Oh, bliss.

That Tucker though. Ha! Wait till I tell Miranda. A nasty sense of humour lurks in that dour shell. Nasty, but delicious. For a man of few words he picks them well. Opened the door to me himself. Stared at the egg-cup while I explained. 'Ay,' he nodded. 'The missus'll have some mustard.' And disappeared inside. Didn't take the egg-cup. Left me standing there, the lunatic from London proffering his dinky begging bowl. Returned with an unopened jar and handed it over, dismissed my thanks. Then walked down to the yard gate with me, as if he didn't trust me to close it properly. How did he get the subject round to those cheeses? God knows. But he did. He and the missus only eat Cheddar, he told me. They gave the cheeses to the dogs. But never again, he said. 'Do make 'em fart,' he said. 'Fart something chronic.' Our food, not even fit for dogs. Hell, and he kept a straight face. They know how to slap you down, hats off to them.

I admire him. With a pound of red meat inside me, I can admire him. Fire and spirit. Flesh and blood. Sly bugger. Ready with the needle like that. Ah, that's what meat does for you. The war engine stoked with real fuel. Can't wait to tell Miranda. In fact, can't wait to see her. Roll on bedtime. She's sleeping with a carnivore tonight.

# THE SPECIAL DAY

Gary couldn't hear what his mother was saying at the front door, but knew it was bad news, from her face as she returned to the kitchen.

'It looks as if you'll have to come with us,' she sighed, walking back to the breakfast washing-up. 'Toby's ill. Oh dear.' She rested her hands on the metal rim of the sink and stood a moment with her back to him, gazing out through the window. 'Never mind,' she said abruptly, turning to give him a short smile. 'It's a lovely pub. Right by a river. If it stays like this we'll be able to sit outside. There'll be lots to look at.'

Gary shrugged and said, 'S'okay Mum.' He was disappointed, but not as much as his mother seemed to be.

His mother's friends were called Peter and Janine and they arrived at twelve. His mother had changed out of trousers into a white sleeveless dress and tied her hair up on top of her head, the way she used to when his father was here and she had gone out with him in the evenings. Gary wondered if Peter and Janine were real friends, because she said, 'Oh my God, they're here!' when the bell rang, and glanced around the flat as if she had lost something.

'I'm afraid Gary'll have to come too,' she said, after she had kissed the woman and smiled at the man. 'He was going to a friend's, but his Mum's just called to say he's ill.'

The man Peter said, 'The more the merrier,' and smiled at Gary pleasantly. Peter was tall, with fair hair that touched his collar at the back. Gary had been told that he was a policeman, but he didn't look at all like the policemen who did the bike tests at school. He was wearing a blue check jacket over a white T-shirt and looked more like someone from an American television programme.

Janine said, 'Hello, Gary', and, 'My, he's grown!' admiringly to his mother. Her hair fell in chestnut curls to bare suntanned shoulders and her dress was bright and swirly. Gary thought she looked a bit like someone from the television too. She held out her arm at waist height. 'When I last saw you you were so high,' she told him, smiling as if they had once been great friends. 'Do you remember?'

Gary shook his head and said no. His mother had said they had met three years ago, when he'd been six, but he didn't recognize her. His mother had also said that Janine was an old school friend, and that she was lucky. This was because she was married to Peter and lived in London, but it had something to do with holidays too, and going abroad, and shopping at a place called Wallis's.

Peter hadn't brought a police car. He had a silver Cavalier estate, a new one, still with plastic covers on the back seats. He said Gary and his mother would melt on them, it being such a hot day, and tugged them off before they climbed in. Gary could see that this was another reason Janine was lucky, having such a big new car.

He sat forward in his seat as they set off, so he could watch Peter drive; he especially liked the way he changed gear, using the heel of his palm against the stubby gear stick, in short, definite movements. On the motorway out of the city Peter drove at exactly seventy miles an hour. Other cars overtook them but he didn't say anything or chase them, though he must have known that they were breaking the law.

'We haven't been out in the country for ages, have we Gary?' said his mother, when the houses ended and yellow fields began. 'I can't remember the last time.'

'I came out with Daddy in the winter,' said Gary. 'We went fishing.'

'That was the reservoir,' his mother said. 'That's not real country.'

Gary saw Janine glance at Peter, and it looked as if perhaps she disagreed with this, but was too polite to say so. Instead she smiled at them over her shoulder and said kindly, 'Well of course you need a car. It's hopeless without a car.'

After the motorway came a main road, with several roundabouts, and then a narrower, twisting road. Janine and his mother started to point at things out of the window and give Peter directions, and seemed to get much more friendly and cheerful. Peter grinned at them and said it was all right and it had come back to him now, and really they were more hindrance than help. Gary could tell that they had all been here before, but not for a long time.

'There it is!' cried Janine triumphantly, as they rounded a bend to see a stone bridge ahead of them, and a black and white building beyond. A sign on a pole said it was the White Rabbit.

'It looks just the same!' His mother peered at the building as they scrunched into the car park. She sounded excited. Peter stopped the car next to three others and everyone got out.

The car park was cut into a bank beside the pub, and Gary had to run up concrete steps to see the river. The water was so still it looked more like a lake: a long thin lake, the bridge at one end and trees at the other, the far side of the pub garden. Above, a white sun scorched down from a hazy, brilliant sky.

'Goodness it's hot,' said Janine, coming up behind him with the others. She plucked at the back of her dress. 'You'd have thought there'd be a breeze, wouldn't you, so close to the sea.'

'Are we near the sea?' asked Gary, and looked around eagerly.

Peter pointed towards the trees. 'It's over there,' he said. 'You can't see it from here. But that's where the river's going.'

'It's so pretty,' sighed his mother, smiling at the water with her head tilted. 'I'm so glad it hasn't changed.'

There were white tables and chairs at the top of the lawn, close to the open pub doors. They walked across the grass to them and Janine and his mother sat down, Janine saying wasn't it wonderfully uncrowded, and of course that was the advantage of coming mid-week. Peter asked everyone what they wanted to drink and went inside. Gary wandered down to the river.

'You be careful now,' his mother called after him.

'Oh, don't worry,' he heard Janine say. 'We used to paddle here. God … do you remember that time … after all those babychams …?' Gary heard his mother laugh.

There were large flat stones at the water's edge, like stepping stones, except they ran beside the water, not across it. Gary walked along them in the direction Peter had said the sea was. He knew rivers flowed to seas, but it would have been difficult to tell with this river, because it moved so slowly. Sometimes it almost looked as if it were flowing the other way, though he knew it couldn't be.

Before he reached the trees he passed a sign stuck in the grass which said *Private Fishing*. He stopped and looked out over the water. Insects darted and hovered over the sunlit surface and, close to the opposite bank, where the shadow of the trees began, the air seethed with midges. Twice he heard tiny plops, and saw circular ripples spread across the bright smoothness. It made him think of his father, and the flick of line across other waters, and summer picnics in the past.

He walked on until he met a barbed wire fence. He could have squeezed by, on the water side, but guessed he wasn't meant to. He turned round and started slowly walking back.

In this direction there seemed rather less of the stones to walk on. This seemed odd; he stopped a moment and squatted down to study the shallows near his feet. The very edge of the water was dusty, close to, as if it had a skin, and a small dead leaf floating on it was completely dry. The dust and leaf moved suddenly towards him, and quivered against his shoe. Gary frowned, stepped back a pace, and watched again.

He wondered if he ought to go and tell his mother that the river was getting bigger. Or whether she would only worry, and say it wasn't safe, and make them go. He stared down at the water again. It was definitely growing, but very slowly. He didn't want to go. He decided it couldn't be dangerous, with so much lawn to swell across, and he needn't say anything yet.

He heard his name called and walked back up to the table. Peter had bought him a glass of lemonade and a packet of crisps. Janine was wearing sunglasses and looked even more like someone from the television. Peter looked less like that now, because he had removed his check jacket.

'Can I take the crisps down to the river, Mum?' Gary asked. He glanced back at the water. From here you couldn't really see that it had grown at all.

His mother said that was a good idea, so he carried the lemonade and crisps down the lawn and settled himself on

*Of Sons and Stars*

his stomach on the grass. The river was still swelling; before his crisp packet was empty the mud and stones in front of him were covered, and the water nudged the first blades of grass.

This seemed an important moment. Gary lowered his chin to the ground, so the grass became huge, a jungle of green, and watched intently. The blades trembled, juddered as they were encircled, then collapsed suddenly, as if trapped in the water's skin, only to rise again a moment later, but swaying and alive-looking now, beneath it. A yellow-and-white daisy head appeared amongst them and winked up at him through the water. Its petals bobbed and waved, more like a bright swimming creature than a flower.

The river crept steadily on, engulfing and transforming; he had to wriggle back twice to keep the crisp packet dry. Then, just after he had found a dead match and stuck it in the ground as a marker, everything slowed down. The water touched it, but only pushed and rocked against it, and came no further.

He heard a sound off to his right, a sound he had never heard before. A rhythmic, creaking, swishing noise, getting louder and closer. It was coming through the air, straight at him. He suddenly saw what it was, and scrambled to his feet. Four enormous white shapes rushed past and crashed into the water.

'Mum!' he called, and ran back towards the table.

His mother and Janine were talking with their backs to him. Peter was sitting the other side of the table, leaning forward on his elbows. He heard Janine say, 'Christ, what a year,' almost angrily, before Peter glanced up and saw him. 'Hello Gary,' he said, and touched Janine's arm.

His mother swung round. 'Hello poppet,' she said brightly. 'That was good timing. We've just got you a sandwich.' She said it as if everyone had been talking about food, although Gary didn't think they had.

Peter leant back in his chair, making it squeak, and surveyed the river. 'Hey,' he said loudly. 'Look at the swans. Handsome beasts, aren't they?'

Everyone turned to look. Gary had known that the crashing white shapes were swans but was glad to hear Peter say it. They seemed much smaller from up here, more like they did in books.

His mother frowned. 'Don't try to feed them, will you Gary. You have to be careful with swans.'

'Okay,' said Gary. It hadn't occurred to him that you could feed swans. He watched them glide away towards the bridge, circle in the blackness beneath it, then drift back again. They looked as if they would be insulted to be thrown crusts, as if they were ducks. He wondered how they had known the moment the river stopped growing, and what they were waiting for. On his back he felt the heat of the sun pulsate, like a countdown to something.

He was struck, suddenly, by a tremendous thought.

'Mum?' he asked, excitement mounting. 'Is it a special day today?'

'What d'you mean, poppet?' She gave a small laugh and looked quickly at the others. 'Well ... I suppose it is a little, coming here ...'

'Not like that,' said Gary impatiently. Janine and Peter smiled. Gary tried to think how to say it. 'I mean more like ... like Christmas ... or ...' It came to him in a rush, '... like on that film, when the sun went black.'

His mother stared at him a moment and then laughed and said, 'Oh Gary, whatever made you think that?' She turned to the others. 'He means an eclipse. No, poppet.' She patted his arm kindly. 'Sorry, nothing like that.'

Gary had been so sure of it, just for those few seconds, that he felt cheated. He picked up the cheese sandwich and walked back down to the water. As he ate he studied the

ground, in case the river had begun to grow again, but it
hadn't; in fact in places he could see wet grass, as if it might
actually have shrunk.

The swans moved closer, and the one nearest him stood
up in the water and flapped its wings. Gary decided he
didn't want to sit down there, and walked away from them,
towards the car park.

There was a white Ford Fiesta parked next to the Cavalier
now. A man with a hot red face was standing beside it,
brushing his arm across the roof. Every so often he flicked
his hand towards the ground, as if he had touched something disgusting. At home Gary and his friends were sometimes told to get out of car parks but he thought it would
be all right to go nearer here, because of the Cavalier. He
went down the steps and a few yards across the gravel could
see it was black dots the man was trying to sweep from the
Fiesta, and that they were all over the Cavalier, too.

A woman and a little girl in a pink sundress came out of
the Ladies at the side of the pub and clacked down the steps
behind him.

'It's covered in bloody ants,' the man said crossly, as they
approached. 'Get in the back quick and don't open the windows.'

The woman said, 'But it'll be like an oven,' in a complaining voice, and then gasped, 'Oh, heavens!' and recoiled
from the car.

'They're bloody swarming,' said the man, opening the
back door and pushing the little girl inside. 'Careful they
don't get in your hair.'

The woman gave a shriek, touched her head, and shut herself hurriedly in the car. The man slammed himself into the
driver's seat and started the engine.

After they had gone Gary walked over and studied the
black dots on the Cavalier. The man was right, they were

ants; only they seemed different, not ordinary ants, some-how. He looked at one closely.

It had wings. They all had wings. He watched an ant alight, and fold the wings stiffly across its back. He thought suddenly of the swelling river, and the circling swans.

Some of the ants flew upwards. He tried to follow them with his eyes but was distracted by dark shapes far above: birds, wheeling and soaring, silhouetted against the blue haze of the sky. He was sure there hadn't been so many birds up there earlier, when they arrived. And now he had seen them he realized that he could hear them, too: the air keened with distant cries, shrill and urgent-sounding.

Watching them made him dizzy so he ran over to the concrete steps and sat down. When he looked up again there seemed more, just in those few seconds, and the whirling seemed more frantic.

Sometimes, he noticed, the birds seemed to fly through shimmering pockets of air. He screwed up his eyes, puzzled, and then spotted a pocket further down: this vibrated more than shimmered, and had vague, ghostly substance, like the tremor of something real, but just invisible. Then his eyes shifted focus to another, closer still, and this time it wasn't a shimmer at all, but a cloud of vibrating speckles, and the speckles were alive, and flying, and he realized that they were ants.

He watched the cloud rise and begin to shimmer, until his eyes hurt against the bright sky. Blinking, he dropped his gaze; and on the concrete beside him spotted a winged ant, barely an arm's length away, emerging from a crevice in the step. It crawled an inch towards him, spread shiny translu-cent wings, and flicked into the air. Another appeared behind it, then two more, then, as if tiny gates had been flung wide, a glistening stream of ants. On shining wings they poured into the hot air, mushrooming to a great swarm

above him. He watched the swarm float upwards, still trailing a column of rising ants, till it became what he had just
seen: a speckled, vibrating cloud.

The stream from the crevice beside him dwindled. He saw
the last stragglers leave; then glanced quickly away, caught
by movement below: another exodus was beginning, from
a crack near his foot.

This time he knew what was going to happen. They were
his ants pouring forth, his swarm aloft, his vibrating, speckled cloud; and, drifting higher, his pocket of shimmering air.
He lost it finally, among the whirling birds.

In triumph he scanned the sky and, through comprehend-
ing eyes now, saw them all. His heart wanted to burst. In
every direction, as far as he could see, the air shimmered
with ants. His mind filled with numbers, millions, billions,
trillions, and still it wasn't enough.

He watched the sky a long time, till his mother and Janine
and Peter came round the side of the pub.

'There you are!' laughed his mother. 'We thought you'd
got fed up and gone home!'

There were almost no ants on the car now, and the birds
were much higher. Gary hoped the grown-ups wouldn't
notice and ask him about it. He didn't want to have to
explain that all the ants in the world had taken flight on new
wings and left the earth. And how the water, and the swans,
and birds above had known, and he had witnessed it.

'You've been ever such a good boy,' said his mother, as
they all walked towards the car. She squeezed him suddenly
and kissed him on the forehead.

Janine grinned at him and hissed, 'Your mother's tiddly.'

Peter snorted, 'Look who's talking,' as he unlocked the car,
and Janine pulled a silly face at him.

Gary realized that it was all right, that no one was going
to notice the ants, or ask him anything. For a moment he

wasn't sure about Peter, because he didn't look tiddly at all, and even brushed a few ants off the windscreen with his hand. But then his mother started saying how wonderful it had been to come here, and how important old friends were, and how it had been like finding her old self again; and Peter turned to smile at her, looking as if she had been saying something sad instead of something happy, and even put a hand on her shoulder and kissed her before she got in the car. It was just a quick kiss, though, on the cheek, not like the kisses Gary's father sometimes gave his friend Marie, and Janine didn't seem to mind, so Gary didn't either. He didn't even mind when Peter said, 'You're a good lad, Gary, your mother thinks the world of you,' as he climbed into the car, though he didn't see how, really, he could know.

'It's been a lovely day,' murmured his mother, when they were back on the motorway and had left the yellow fields behind. Her arm was around him and she was staring out of the side window, into the city. She sighed and turned back to him with a smile. 'Sorry about no eclipse,' she said.

Gary smiled back and said, ''S okay, Mum.'

# THE RULES OF A MAN'S LIFE

This was Simon's dream: he was in his car, alone, in a traffic jam on the motorway. It was daylight, a hot cloudless afternoon, and the cars were on a gentle upward gradient. He was trapped in the middle lane, which scarcely seemed to move at all; to either side of him traffic occasionally slid past, at variable speeds, making him feel giddy and disorientated.

The vehicle directly in front of him was a petrol tanker. Its size contributed to his disorientation, as the circular shape of the tank filled the windscreen and gave him nothing distant to fix on. The tank bore a huge logo, which for some reason he could never remember after waking, except that it was red. The vehicle itself was white.

He would become aware, first, of a shimmer between the rear of the tanker and his own car bonnet, which seemed merely a localized indication of the day's heat. But then he would smell a familiar, dangerous smell. And then he would see the petrol, leaking from a metal hose the size of a vacuum cleaner hose, projecting from the base of the tank. The petrol was leaking from the chained cap. Sometimes merely a drip, sometimes a trickle, sometimes a splash. The shimmer was petrol vapour. But most was spilling on to the tarmac. It trailed, it must, under his car. And under the one behind, and the one behind that.

There was no escape. No one else could see the leaking petrol. He was too close to the tanker to move left or right out of the lane. Even if the tanker moved a short way on and he tried indicating left or right, no one, he knew, would let him in.

This was the climax of the dream. It would linger just long enough for him to contemplate the terror of a spark, a hot exhaust, a tossed cigarette stub. And then he would wake.

Simon did not need an analyst to tell him what the dream was about. He knew that in adulthood nightmares were pathological, and were usually caused by feelings of power-lessness. In his case, he dreamed this dream, he knew, because he hated his job.


He hadn't always; twenty years ago, he had taken pride in it. 'A perfectionist', he was called, and he liked the term; it seemed flattering. In those days, as an Assistant Estates Officer in his north London housing department, he would be given a task – which would be well within his capabilities – and would execute it as perfectly, as conscientiously, as he knew how. He believed in the maxim: if a job's worth doing, it's worth doing well. How things had changed. Public housing had taken a battering in the two decades since. He had been promoted several times and his staff – half the number he'd have had as a manager in the old days – did the hands-on work. He delegated. There was no time for perfection. There was no possibility of perfection. No one expected it. But knowing this did not console him. There was no pleasure in just-good-enough management, just-passable work, and he was not a natural delegator. Mistakes distressed him. He felt responsible. He was responsible.

He was already taking beta-blockers, and he was only forty-two. They kept his heart steady, warded off the panic.

They didn't heal the frustrations, right the incompetences, or alter his distress at them, but they stopped his heart breaking, physically, over them.

To take drugs, though, was a sign of failure. He had to acknowledge it: he was a failure. That he had chosen the path he had, and not made a success of it, was difficult to bear. The blackness of this – the twenty years behind him, perhaps twenty more in front – threatened to suffocate him at night. He would dream his nightmare. Wake with a sense of impending catastrophe, which would stay with him for days. His doctor said the feeling was a well-documented phenomenon. He was a mite depressed too, perhaps, as well as anxious.

He remembered sometimes, with astonishment, the early seventies, his years at university. The world of work then, it seemed, had been simply one of several options. When – if – you opted for it, you could dip your career toes into a pool, lift them out if things didn't suit, and dip them elsewhere. Between pools, you could play around. There was plenty of time. Work wasn't everything.

Oh, how wrong, how naïve, how arrogant, even, they had been. They thought the world had changed. That they, indeed, had changed it. Not until they were up to their knees did they feel the mud. The clinging, sucking hold of it. By then it was too late.

His wife Christine once said,'Why too late?' and angered him with her lack of understanding. They had a mortgage, a teenage son and daughter, elderly parents, responsibilities; how dare she say it.

But then, Christine thought he was in the wrong job. He should have been a craftsman, according to her. He was good with his hands. He understood the physical world. The craft world still valued perfection.

And she told him that he was not alone. That the world

groaned with men unhappy in their work. She told him
about husbands of women friends: Alex, who drank far too
much, and would one day kill himself, or someone else,
drunk-driving. Fergus, who had nightmares more alarming
than Simon's, during which he would sleep-walk, punch
furniture, and shout obscenities into doorways. Paul, who
already had a stomach ulcer, and dangerously high blood
pressure.

These stories bewildered Simon. It seemed to him that he
and his wife inhabited different worlds. In hers men were
vulnerable, their lives often problematic and stress-laden,
and there was no shame – for anyone – in acknowledging
this. The straitjacket of a man's life – the expectations of that
life – was the villain.

In Simon's own world, these vulnerable men were invisible. Men – other men, that is – were strong. There were
rules. Men competed. Men provided. Men succeeded. Their
weaknesses were risen above. Or hidden. He hid his own.

His wife did not exhort him to give up his job – she
understood the terrors of joblessness in the nineties – but
nor did she exhort him not to. She behaved as if the decision
was his. From time to time she would prompt him to think
about it, with remarks such as,'I worry about you,' or
'retraining is possible, you know,' or 'we'd manage if you
gave up, people do.' Christine had changed her own job
twice after returning to full-time work. But then women
were freer. With a husband behind them, they could afford
to take risks. He couldn't. The straitjacket held him tight.
The rules of a man's life. Despite the nightmares, despite the
night suffocations, despite the sense of catastrophe to come.


But when it happened, it happened not to him, but to one
of his oldest friends. To Julian, suddenly cut down one late

February day, by a massive, fatal cardiac arrest. Julian was not one of the problematic men. He was one of the ebullient, successful, unarguably happy men.

When Simon heard the news over the telephone, he felt sick. The sort of nausea that goes with knowing that there has been a terrible mistake. He experienced it, to a lesser degree, at work, when crises were reported to him. He told Christine, who burst violently into tears. 'Poor Alice!' she wept. 'Oh, those poor, poor children!' Simon couldn't cry. His only, overwhelming, thought was: they have taken the wrong man.

The following Friday he and Christine drove the hundred miles north to Halesowen, Birmingham for the funeral. Their children, who were friends with Alice and Julian's children, came too. On the way Simon's daughter said 'You realize this is the first funeral I've been to,' and Simon said, 'I suppose it must be.' The remark stayed in his mind and after a while he realized that this funeral was a first for him, too. The first where he would be mourning someone he cared deeply about. He had, to date, lost no parents, no close family, no close friends. He had never before felt bereaved.

The funeral was held at a crematorium at the edge of a tree-fringed park. Julian had led a successful life; now his wife, with the help of friends, laid on a successful funeral. Julian had not been religious, and God was not mentioned. But love, celebration, the agony of loss, and the promise of immortality were. Scott Holland, Shakespeare and Rossetti were read. There were heartfelt personal tributes. The immediate family did not cry – it was too early for them, Simon supposed – but others did. Christine and both his children wept. Simon couldn't. He was appalled by the wrongness of it all. There, in the coffin in front of them, was the dead body of his friend. Around the coffin, his friend's shell-shocked family. Julian was irretrievable. He had lived his life, had his chance, and was gone for ever. In Simon's mind a slow terror began to build.

It was still with him, though muted, when they left the emotional gathering at Alice's house. It was six-thirty, and quite dark. He offered to drive home; something to occupy his thoughts.

'Maybe we should have left it a while,' Christine said, as they joined the packed carriageway of the M5. 'Oh dear.'

Simon knew, the moment he saw the traffic, that he had made a colossal mistake. He should have known. The terror mounted. His mouth was sticky dry.

After a few minutes of crawling progress Christine said, 'You're very quiet,' in a coded voice, as if she guessed something was wrong, and he managed to say 'Yes'. It wasn't fair that his family were here. In the dream, he had always been alone.

The traffic slowed to a halt, as he knew it would. He was, inevitably, in the middle lane. Brake lights spattered the windscreen red. There was a lorry in front. He crept up behind it. It was not a petrol tanker, but a goods lorry. On the tall rectangular back, white letters on green said: *Eezybeds - The Perfect Night's Sleep*. A mattress lorry.

Dreams did not come true. No. They came in disguise. Simon's hands were wet on the steering wheel. The lorry moved forwards a few yards. But the lanes either side were stationary now. He had his family with him. They were all trapped.

He glanced sideways and caught his wife's profile, illuminated in the brake light glow. Red for danger; splashed all over his wife and children.

His mind suddenly opened. Rules did not have to be obeyed. The realization was there, full beam, in his mind. He could save his family.

He indicated left, and swung the front wing of the car,

very assertively, into the slow lane. It was just moving again now. A couple of cars steered around it; the third hung back and flashed him in. It was as easy as that. But now he had got this far, he would take them right out of danger. He kept the indicator going, and moved onto the hard shoulder.

'What are you doing?' Christine was alarmed. 'Is something wrong with the car? For God's sake!'

His son removed the Walkman from his ears and said warningly, 'Hey, Dad!'

'Be quiet. Please.' He was in control. The Frankley services were less than a mile ahead.

He trundled the car along the hard shoulder, praying that they would meet no obstacles. They were undertaking everyone. What he was doing was risky, and against the law, but it was possible. Escape was possible.

Christine's body was rigid beside him. Several cars flashed them. But there were no obstructions. Nothing to stop them. Then they were at the mouth of the services access road. He turned into it. He heard Christine expel a hissing breath.

He parked in front of the brightly-lit Granada service building. Christine turned round to the children and said in a steady, ordinary voice, 'We'll wait here an hour or so. You fancy chips?' and both the children said,'Yeah!'

They got out. Simon watched them walk towards the entrance and then forced himself to get out too and followed them into the building. He went straight to the Gents, locked himself in one of the cubicles, and leant back against the dividing wall. He thought he was going to cry now, in earnest, but he didn't. His eyes wetted, that was all.

When his feelings of shame and relief had died down – to think that for all these years, he thought he'd been protecting his family – he let himself out, washed his face, and rejoined them in the cafeteria.

# JAMES

1963. The summer of the Great Train Robbery, and the Profumo affair. The summer I was thirteen. And a summer, for my mother, my brother and myself, of perpetual holiday, because we were between homes – my doctor father had just changed jobs – and renting Ashgrove.

Ashgrove was a dark ramshackle house in the middle of a Sussex wood; fingers of overgrown coppice tapped our windows at night. When the sun shone only small pools of sunlight made it through the leaf canopy. In the daytime the air within and around the house throbbed, as the house had no mains electricity and was powered by a generator in the cellar, which was turned off at night; we all had torches beside our beds.

Staying with us – because my father was at his hospital job all day, and my mother would never holiday alone – was Aunt Louise, who wasn't a real aunt, but my mother's oldest and best friend, and Louise's two children, Patrick and Maddy. Patrick was eight, and company for my younger brother William, and Maddy was eleven, and company for me. Maddy and Patrick's father had died of septicaemia after a tooth operation when Patrick was one, so Louise was a widow, but no longer an unhappy widow. That summer she brought her own friend with her. James.

That's what we called him: James, Louise's friend. He was a university student who had been lodging in her London house, and much younger than her. All the other grown-ups could remember the war, and he couldn't – I remember Aunt Louise teasing him about it. But we all liked him, in the way you like friendly, attractive pets. Everyone touched him. It was impossible not to when you were close to him and he teased you, or grinned at you, saying or doing something provocative, or silly. Your hands just reached out, smacking, or pushing away, as they would with a playful dog. Even my father occasionally patted him, in a manly way – more light punches really – when he and James passed in doorways, perhaps, or met on the stairs.

Having him with us altered things, though. For the better, mostly; only at one time of day was I unsure of this: the early evenings, when my father returned from work. We would see his Austin approaching down the drive and somehow the holiday atmosphere would falter. My father would come in, suited and formal from the hospital, and my mother and Louise would flutter around him, pampering him with drinks, asking him about his day, and James would retreat, silent and smiling, to the edge of rooms, the walls behind sofas. I was reminded uncomfortably of school, when teachers interrupted us girls at play. Though when my father left the room to go upstairs and change, nobody caught anyone else's eye, or smirked behind their hands. And by supper time the atmosphere would have relaxed, my father would have slotted back into our holiday world, and the grown-ups would talk and laugh together then, over wine and food and coffee. James would re-emerge from the background, telling funny stories, and entertaining us. Often he waited on us, looking quite professional, a white napkin draped over his arm. And sometimes he cooked. I had never seen a man cook before, and the first time I saw James cutting up vegetables and stirring saucepans I thought some catastrophe must have happened, though of course it hadn't. His efforts seemed to hugely amuse my mother and Louise. They somehow flattered my father, too, elevating him above such domesticity.

Nearly every day Louise took my mother out in her car, house hunting. Maddy and I quickly gave up going with them; we were too uncritical. All the houses we looked at seemed perfect. I'd cry, 'This could be my room!' or, 'Oh, can we live here, Mummy?' and my mother would murmur, 'Ssh, dear,' sounding embarrassed. She didn't seem to like any of the houses – or perhaps she just enjoyed house hunting. But anyway, if we went, James couldn't go too, because of leaving the boys. And although James was always willing to babysit, and the boys loved fighting him and tying him up and making him surrender, Louise wanted him with her. So when Maddy and I announced that we were fed up with trips to houses that we knew we were never going to buy, my mother was delighted, and from then on she and Louise and James did the house hunting, and Maddy and I stayed behind.

That was when we started to play in the shed in the woods. This shed was only a hundred yards from the house but hidden by the trees, and it was about the size of a garage or loose box but can't have been either, because it had an ordinary twist handle door. The inside was empty except for six straw bales stacked against the end wall and, beside them, a pile of empty folded hessian sacks. The floor was concrete and there were two side windows, glazed, with chicken wire protecting the glass.

Maddy and I decided to transform the shed into a house. Our very own house. Maddy loved house games. I usually preferred horse games, but preparing a house is much like preparing a stable, so I was just as keen. Over two days we

swept out the whole of the interior: the ribbed roof of cob-
webs, the wooden walls of dust and sawdust and woodlice,
and the floor of everything we'd brushed down, plus blown-
in leaves and wisps of straw. We removed the chicken wire
and cleaned the window glass. The shed was suddenly twice
as light. We had the hessian sacks and the straw, too – the
raw materials for a bed, or at least somewhere to lie down –
so we dragged three of the bales outside and split them; the
plumped-up straw filled nine bags. We tied their necks with
baler twine and piled them back into the hut, and then lay
side by side on them until they settled into a mattress.

On the third day we realized that our new house had
even got its own pet. On our arrival first thing we dis-
turbed a ginger tomcat, curled up on one of the remaining
straw bales. The cat eyed us glassily before shooting past our
legs out of the open door. We puzzled over how it had got in,
until the next morning, closing the door quickly behind us –
Maddy had fantasies of taming our visitor – it escaped by
squeezing itself almost flat and disappearing through the
three inch gap at the bottom of the door.

Still, even if the cat wasn't friendly, he was a domestic
presence. We lay on our backs on our sack bed, now covered
with a picnic rug, and played 'what-if' games. Our favourite
was to imagine what we'd do if we were suddenly presented
with a million pounds; this was the minimum the train
robbers had got away with the week before. Everyone was
still talking about the robbery, and the amount they'd stolen
seemed to get bigger every day. For some reason, although
my parents usually disapproved of robbers, they hadn't
sounded particularly disapproving of this robbery, even
though a train driver had been hurt. They had sounded
astonished at first, and then, when the amount of cash stolen
was announced, and the fact that it was only government
money, and no one would really miss it, almost admiring.

Louise had groaned, 'My God, a million ... Maybe two ...' and pretended to swoon against James.

Maddy wanted to buy houses, of course, with her million. The houses my mother was looking at cost about eight thousand, so Maddy reckoned she could buy dozens for herself, all over the world, and furnish them as extravagantly as she liked. Everywhere she went, she would have a home to stay in. I planned to buy myself a horse, an Arab stallion, and was torn between also buying an island – with a sandy coastline that my stallion could gallop around – or investing in a large slice of Canada. I was reading Mazo de la Roche at the time, and besotted with the place. I thought horses would like it too.

The sack bed was cosy and comfortable and our next ambition was to spend the night in the shed. We thought of asking permission from the grown-ups – who would probably have agreed – but decided not to, because if the boys knew we were sleeping out they would want to too, and that would spoil everything. The grown-ups didn't yet know that we'd made a home of the shed, and although the boys knew we played in it, we'd never let them see what we'd done inside.

The next day we bought spare batteries for our torches from the village shop and in the afternoon took our eiderdowns and pillows out, so we wouldn't have to struggle with them in the dark. The planning felt exciting but not especially naughty; we'd camped out alone, with grown-up approval, several times on other holidays. We had to carry the bedding out the front door because James was sunbathing on a rug in a small patch of sunlight near the kitchen door, with his shirt off. Normally both Maddy and I liked talking to him and he probably wouldn't have asked about the bedding – the boys were always taking sheets and blankets outside for their games – but somehow he looked different half naked and we both, without discussing it, chose to avoid him.

When we came in for tea he was still there; I could see him from the kitchen window, lying on his side on the rug with his eyes closed. Where the sun's rays caught the edge of his back and shoulder his skin seemed to glow, as if he was lit from inside. I was meant to be calling people in and I said, looking at him, 'I think James is asleep.'

My mother came over to the window and stared out at James. Then her lips twitched to a small smile and she said, 'I doubt it. I expect he knows he looks pretty like that.'

I was embarrassed. I felt my mother had forgotten who she was talking to. I'd never heard a man called 'pretty' before. It seemed to insult James. And for some reason it brought to mind an image of the two young women we kept seeing on the television, Christine Keeler and Mandy Rice-Davies. The television and newspapers said that they were pretty too, in a way that definitely insulted them. Christine Keeler's friend Mr Ward had only just killed himself because of the horrible things they said.

That night, after the generator thrum had stopped and we'd heard the last bedroom door close – James's, next to ours – Maddy and I lit our torches, put on our sandshoes and dressing gowns, and crept downstairs. We let ourselves out of the back door, which was never locked, and picked our way through the trees towards the shed. The grass was wet and our sandshoes became instantly cold and clammy. Outside the shed door we sang a couple of quiet verses of *The Night has a Thousand Eyes* because it was our favourite song that summer and we could see thousands of stars in a gap of sky above us. Then we went into the hut, kicked off our shoes, and climbed onto our straw-sack bed.

Once we were comfortable and had swung the light beams around a few times, just to fix our bearings, we switched the torches off. The scent of shed became intense. A raw, saw-dusty, damp smell. We were quiet for a little while, but not drowsily quiet, and then Maddy asked if I thought her mother and James were having sexual intercourse.

I was the expert on sex, because I was older than Maddy, and the daughter of a doctor. I had had years of access, in our last house, to bound, attic-stored copies of *The Lancet*. I knew the human body – or at least the diseased human body – literally inside and out. I had seen a photograph of a man with elephantiasis of his testicles.

In the darkness I considered Maddy's question, trying to imagine Aunt Louise and James having intercourse; and then said no. Because, if they'd wanted to, they'd be married. The two went together. When you wanted to have sexual intercourse with someone, you married them. If you could. Mr Profumo hadn't been able to marry Christine Keeler because he was already married, and the same was true, pre-sumably, for the Russian diplomat who'd also had inter-course with her. But if people could get married, they would. It was immoral not to. And Aunt Louise could have got married to James, but had chosen not to. Therefore, I con-cluded, she wasn't having sexual intercourse with him.

It occurred to me suddenly, though I didn't say anything to Maddy, that my father might have his suspicions about Louise and James. Or anxieties, anyway. That this might explain why the atmosphere was always slightly awkward when he got back from work. He was responsible for Aunt Louise while she was staying with us. Men were responsible for women in their household. Like Mr Ward had been for Christine Keeler.

Maddy was pleased that I didn't think her mother and James were lovers. I could hear the relief in her voice. It was difficult to imagine parents – or any grown-ups, really – having sexual intercourse, and quite hard to talk about, even with Maddy, whom I knew so well. So we didn't pursue the subject. We talked about spending our millions instead, and eventually fell asleep.

When I woke it was light and I was itching unbearably around my waist. I had to scratch, and woke Maddy. Something had happened to her too – one of her eyelids was hugely swollen. I threw off the eiderdown and saw two specks jump from my pyjamas on to the picnic rug. I knew immediately what they were – cat fleas.

I had fifteen bites, eleven around my waist and four in a line above my elbow. Maddy only had nine, but they were across her shoulder and face. We guessed that we hadn't been bitten before, during the day, because we hadn't lain down long enough for our warmth to draw the insects up to us, and because we'd worn more clothes. We thought most of the fleas would be back below the hessian now, but we took the eiderdown and pillows outside anyway, shook them, and draped them over tree branches. Fleas, I knew, didn't like the cold. It was only six o'clock, and the air very chilly.

We left the bedding there for half an hour and still had plenty of time to get back to our bedrooms before anyone else woke. At breakfast we told the grown-ups that a mosquito had droned around our room before we'd gone to sleep – and look, it had bitten Maddy badly on the face. I wore a long-sleeved shirt so my upper arms were covered. My mother gave Maddy a tube of caladryl ointment and we took it upstairs and plastered ourselves with the pink chalky cream.

At lunch, because we knew we wouldn't be sleeping out again, and therefore no longer needed to keep anything secret, we told the grown-ups about tidying up the shed. They weren't going anywhere in the afternoon, so once the washing-up was done they walked into the woods to see what we'd done.

Louise squealed with enthusiasm at our rug-covered bed.

Or sofa, as we now called it. She lifted the rug, patted the hessian admiringly, and cried, 'How clever, girls! A nest!'

At that, James flung himself full-length on his back across the bed, folded his arms under his head, and grinned up at my mother and Louise. It was such an impulsive action, not like an adult at all. I couldn't imagine my father doing it. My mother turned away and said to Maddy and me, 'My, you must have been busy,' looking charmed at what we'd done, and offered us one of the coffee tables from the house. Then Patrick and William came roaring through the door, threw themselves on top of James, and tried to tickle him to death. Louise helped by pinning his arms down, while my mother stood watching with a broad smile on her face. Maddy and I went outside and left them to it; we thought they were all being rather silly, and making a mess of our work.

When they'd gone we tidied up and swept the floor, and then picked flowers, mostly everlasting sweet peas, which grew in drifts around the back kitchen door, and put them in a pewter vase on the coffee table my mother had brought across. She also gave us some green patterned material left over from making a skirt which we cut up and tacked above the windows as curtains, tying them back with string.

My father came home early that afternoon and I caught him before he went into the house and took him down to see the shed too. It was suddenly important to me that he should see everything that the other grown-ups had seen. Inside the shed he stooped to smell the flowers on the table. He looked so handsome in his dark suit that he made the hut look shabby. I wanted to ask him to try the sofa, but realized he couldn't, dressed like that.

We walked back with him to the house and Louise greeted him in the hall. James was hovering behind her. From my father's side I seemed to see them very clearly; I hadn't noticed before how Louise squirmed when she talked to him, and I wanted to tell her to stand still, and not treat my father like an outsider. Behind her, James had become almost invisible. It was odd, but my father seemed to swell beside me; he seemed even more adult and in charge than usual.

That night he refused a drink and didn't change his suit. He'd come back for supper, but had to return to the hospital afterwards. This happened occasionally; he finished so late that he was given a room in the doctors' residences to sleep in.

We ate as usual at seven and half-way through the meal Maddy interrupted the grown-ups' conversation to ask Aunt Louise what a call-girl was. There'd been a television programme on earlier about Mr Profumo's resignation.

Louise looked at the other grown-ups and said that a call-girl was someone you could ring up and pay to be your girl-friend.

'But,' said Maddy, frowning, 'how can anyone be two people's girl-friend?'

'Ah,' said Louise. 'Well, obviously not at the same time.'

'But Mr Profumo and that Russian man were,' complained Maddy. 'I heard them say so. That's why Mr Profumo resigned.'

The boys goggled at Louise, waiting for her reply. My father leant forward.

'No,' he said. 'Mr Profumo resigned because he lied to Parliament about what he was doing. Because lying is dishonourable.'

It seemed to me that a lie couldn't possibly be as dishonourable as sharing a girl-friend with another man while you were already married; but grown-ups often seemed to have strange priorities. And to be amazingly naïve. I mean, who wouldn't lie in those circumstances?

James said, 'Mr Profumo and Ivanov didn't see Christine Keeler at *exactly* the same time, Maddy. She's just a girl who had several boyfriends.'

Louise snorted and my father said, 'I think that's enough.' James caught his eye and nodded. Louise and my mother exchanged quick grins. James jumped up and got another bottle of cider for them and himself, and we started talking about other things.

After supper we children were allowed to watch the sitting-room television while the grown-ups carried on talking in the kitchen. We watched *No Hiding Place* and then my father came in to say goodnight, and we heard the back door slam and his Austin crunch down the drive. We watched some more television and I knew it must be past the boys' bedtime, but the others were still talking and laughing loudly in the kitchen.

In the end I went through to remind them. They were all sitting along one side of the big kitchen table with glasses in front of them. James was in the middle and I saw Louise's head lift from his shoulder as I came in. My mother was holding James's hand on the table in front of her, palm upwards, as if she was reading his fortune. She jumped up and cried, 'My goodness, the boys!' and Louise moaned, 'Oh God, the boys, yes,' and became all floppy and giggly. James didn't move or say anything at all. He had a bright pink spot on each cheek and his eyes were fierce and dreamy at the same time. He looked like someone who has been told something amazing, and can't quite believe it.

The boys were sent to bed and soon afterwards Maddy and I went up too. We didn't say goodnight to the grown-ups, we just went. I lay awake for a long time after Maddy had dropped off, because my bites were hot and itching. I heard the generator turned off, a distant vibration suddenly stop. Then nothing.

In the middle of the night I was woken by something. A voice: a faraway, shouting, man's voice. Not loud at all, but frightening, because it was angry. I was instantly wide awake. And then I heard a thin high wail behind the man's voice, like an animal cry. Except it wasn't.

I sat up in bed. The house seemed absolutely still. I whispered, 'Maddy?' but got no reply. I could hear her snuffly breathing. And I could still hear the man's voice. I got out of bed, tiptoed to the bedroom door, and opened it.

The blackness outside the door was thick and silent. The voice wasn't in the house. I closed the door again, padded across to the window, and opened it wide. The trees outside creaked at me. The shouting was still distant, but louder now, and a point of light flickered far away in the blackness. Someone was down there, with a torch, behind the trees.

Then I heard, very clearly, a woman's voice. I didn't want to recognize it, but I couldn't help it. It was Aunt Louise's. I heard her cry, 'Leave him alone, Graham. Please. Just leave him,' and then her voice became a sob. And then I heard the sound of something, or someone, being pushed, or falling, into undergrowth.

Graham was my father's name. I didn't want to hear any more. I was terrified that Maddy might wake. Quickly, but very carefully, I pulled the window tight shut and ran back to bed. I waited, straining to hear, until a door slammed downstairs. Then I tugged the blankets up over my head.

I knew what had happened. Aunt Louise and James had been in our shed. My father had come back unexpectedly and found them. I knew why he was so angry, what Louise and James had been doing. I couldn't say it to myself, and I couldn't see it in my mind. But I still knew. The nearest I could get was to see another picture, of James as I'd seen him that afternoon, lying on his back on our shed sofa-bed, his arms behind his head, grinning up at us. And my mother's voice was there somewhere too, with its mocking edge, saying, 'He knows he looks pretty like that.'

I thought I wouldn't be able to go back to sleep. But suddenly it was light, and Aunt Louise was in the room. She was bending over Maddy's bed and whispering, 'Darling, darling, wake up. You have to get up now.'

Maddy said, 'Wha … wha … ' half rising, and Louise put her finger to her lips and said, 'Ssh … I'll tell you down-stairs. Breakfast is ready.'

I sat up. Louise turned round and with her mouth trying to smile said, 'We have to go. Something's happened. I'm so sorry.' Her voice cracked. She got up from Maddy's bed, and left us.

We got dressed. I didn't say anything to Maddy about what I'd heard in the night. Downstairs the boys were already up, sitting at the kitchen table circling spindles of golden syrup onto their cornflakes. My mother and Louise were talking in low voices in the scullery. The Austin was outside the win-dow, but there was no sign of my father. I guessed he was still upstairs. There was no sign of James, either.

Then I heard Louise cry, almost a wail, 'Oh God, oh God, these bites,' and caught a glimpse of her pulling up the front of her blouse. Round her midriff were huge red lumps, just like my flea-bite lumps. From the shed sofa-bed, I knew.

Maddy lifted her head from her cereal, her eyes still stupid with sleep, and asked, 'Where's James? Is he coming back with us?'

Louise tucked her blouse into her waistband again, and came over to us. 'Yes,' she said. 'He's having his breakfast in the sitting-room. But leave him alone, please, Maddy. And you, Patrick,' she added sharply, as Patrick half rose. 'I mean it.'

After breakfast Louise went upstairs and packed Maddy's suitcase, then Patrick's, and carried them both down. The door of the sitting-room was closed and none of us children dared open it. Louise brought a tartan suitcase downstairs which Maddy said was James's. My mother helped stack all their luggage in the hall, ready to load in Louise's car.

I got the feeling, watching Aunt Louise and my mother work, and imagining James, isolated and silent in the sitting-room, that he had become one of us children. A child who had done something so wicked that we weren't allowed to associate with him.

Louise loaded the car with the suitcases and then hustled Maddy and Patrick outside and into the back. Maddy looked confused. She said, 'Mummy, are we coming here again?' and Louise shook her head fast and said, 'No dear, I'm sorry, please be quiet.'

And then my mother came out of the house with James. He was holding a white folded cloth in his hand and as he passed me he touched it to his right eye, which was purple, as if he'd squashed a blackberry in it. He held himself stiffly, and although my mother's manner was kind it came to me that he hated her. That indeed, this morning, he hated all of us. So, watching him, I hated him back, for spoiling our holiday, and making Aunt Louise take Maddy away. My father was right; everything had to be James's fault.

Louise got into the driver's seat and started the engine, and the car moved off down the drive. We watched it trundle round the first corner and then it was gone. All we could hear were the trees rustling and creaking and the distant thrum of the generator in the cellar.

My mother put her arm around me and murmured, 'It's all right, dear, it's all right now,' and her body heaved in a sigh. Then she pulled away, turned to face the house, and pushed her sleeves up her arms. It was a gesture of resignation, disaster put behind her, girding up for the new. An unremarkable picture, you'd think – mother at doorway, drama over – but one that is still clear, even now, in my mind. What children cannot make sense of they overlook or dismiss at the time, but store away for later. Because they know, deep inside, what is important.

And that is why I can still see my mother standing there at Ashgrove's front door, her body slack from her sigh, her sleeves rolled to her elbows; and why I can still see the pale undersides of her forearms, studded with the angry, scarlet, swellings of cat–flea bites.

# BLUE PASTEL WOMAN

Let me describe the picture. It is of a young, naked woman lying on her side on a sheeted double bed. She is propped on one elbow, her body facing us. Her thighs and lower legs are together, her knees slightly bent. A touch of mermaid.

The picture was drawn twenty-four years ago, in dark blue pastel on a large sheet of white cartridge paper. Pastels or charcoals were the young artist's favourite medium – they suited his cavalier, broad-stroke, almost slapdash style – but neither artist nor model can remember now why blue was chosen. Very possibly, since at the time the artist only drew for pleasure, having abandoned formal training some years before, the blue was simply one of the few sticks in the pastel box left unbroken, or of sufficient length to use. Whatever the reason, it is a strong, attractive blue, not at all cold, and can be seen now, since blue is the colour of time, to have been a good choice.

So; the model lies across the bed at an oblique angle to the artist, her head nearest him, her body trailing away from left to right. Her naked figure is sketched with great confidence and conviction down to her knees, but beyond this we sense the artist's interest flag; the model's furthest extremities, her toes, are only cursorily sketched, with wrist-flicks of short blue lines. A suggestion of fused fin, almost, rather than feet, reinforcing the lower-body mermaid impression.

Although the model, overall, is average sized, with a flat young woman's abdomen and slender arms, her breasts are large. They are pendulous and look soft and round and entirely natural. The model remembers being told by a male acquaintance, some time before this picture was drawn, that the perfect female breast fitted exactly inside a champagne glass. She remembers mocking this pronouncement. The breasts in the picture are more wassail-cup than champagne-glass sized. You sense however that whatever ideals may have prevailed when the picture was drawn – and a boyish skinniness was undoubtedly fashionable then – the artist had no reservations about the size or shape of his model's breasts. The model, even after twenty-four years, can remember her own youthful body and admires the accuracy of his drawing. We feel, indeed, quite strongly, from the centre-stage position given to the woman's upper torso, that both artist and model must have been comfortable with the flesh as it was.

The model's face, interestingly, is not visible. She is looking away from us, towards a point somewhere the other side of the curved mound of her hips. Towards her left arm, perhaps, which is draped across a sketchily-drawn plumped-up pillow behind her. All we see of her above the shoulders is her hair: thick, long, ungroomed tresses, possibly fair, which fall almost to the point of her supporting elbow. It is the clumped, slightly damp-looking hair of someone who has just woken, or just bathed, or, possibly, just unentwined herself from someone else.

We know the model is aware of being drawn, because of her arranged, mermaid-like pose, and there is, therefore, despite her turned-away gaze, no sense of voyeurism in the picture. What we do sense is that the model felt no need to watch the artist at work, or, indeed, attend to the creative process at all, as if she trusted the artist and her body to have a direct rapport, without mediation or supervision by herself. And as if confident that between them, left alone, body and artist were capable of capturing and expressing the whole of her. Perhaps the picture, para-doxically, expresses more for the very lack of a face. Faces are never blank slates and always attract the eye. This body expresses total ease, precisely, one feels, because it does not watch the artist, and its focus is diffuse. And the artist, for his part, draws what he sees, under no one else's eye, as and how he pleases.

This drawing, though it has existed for twenty-four years, has been viewed by no one except artist and model. It has never been mounted or hung, and although it has charm it is of no artistic merit. Neither artist nor model, at the time, expected otherwise. It was the act of drawing the picture that was the event; the pastel-on-paper result was merely the memento of that event. And the drawing only exists now for the same reason that any household memorabilia exist: it was durable, has been kept in a sensible place, and no accident has befallen it. And, of course, no one has been moved to deliberately destroy it. Deliberate destruction would be meaningful in a way that simple retention isn't.

So where is it now, this drawing? Well, this picture, of a young woman lying naked on her first marital bed, sketched by her young husband one hothouse afternoon twenty-four years ago, is kept, along with other early sketches, under the same couple's present marital bed. The couple did not put it there for any significant, symbolic reason; the floor under the king-sized divan was simply a safe, convenient spot for storing a large, flat, rarely-opened portfolio.

Nevertheless, both artist and model know that the picture is there. And because they know this, just occasionally, while lying above it, they recall it. The blue pastel image has taken on, these days, in both their minds, a talisman quality. A quality never intended, but perhaps inevitable. It has been a long time. The artist, over the years, has forgotten how to draw. The model is no longer longhaired, or youthful. And yet the originals are still there, underneath; look, there is proof: blue pastel woman and her artist, not an arm's length away.

# THE BEGINNING OF SOMETHING

Kay and her son stood facing into the wind, looking out over the broad plain of the Usk Valley. They were taking a Saturday morning walk high on the side of the Blorenge Mountain.

'How's the head now?' Kay asked.

Alex frowned, as if he needed to consult internally before replying, then nodded and said, 'Better.' His long dark hair was tied back into a pony-tail, but several wisps had broken free and were feathered by the breeze against his cheekbones. He still looked pale and hung-over. Kay regarded him unsympathetically. She had had a late night too, lying awake rigid in her bed, waiting for his return from town. But, looking at him, she was nevertheless conscious of savouring the moment: today would be the last occasion, for a good while, that she would be able to look at him. Tomorrow he left Wales. Tomorrow his father would drive him to Colchester, and he would start life as an undergraduate.

She said this quite easily to herself. She faced the thought of losing him with equanimity. This morning, almost with relief.

Alex walked on, a yard or so in front of her. The track that circled the humping summit of the mountain was narrow, fringed with brown dead-head clumps of August-flowered heather. Here and there a hint of purple lingered on.

The boy stopped again and fixed his eyes on the view. 'You won't ever move, will you?'

Kay drew level. 'Well. The house will be rather big for us now.'

'I mean from here. From this.' He nodded outwards.

Kay looked across the pastoral fields of the Usk floodplain, towards the Black Mountain horizon. Today, for once, where passing cloud shadow fell on dark upland bracken, the mountains did look black.

'You want to keep a stake in this, do you?'

Alex nodded. 'I can't imagine living where there aren't mountains. Be weird.'

'That's because you were born here,' Kay said. 'Mountains are like the sea. They imprint on the soul.'

Alex turned to look at her. 'You're not going to move house, are you? My room ... you said ...'

Kay smiled. 'I won't touch a thing.' She knew it wouldn't matter if she did. Alex just wanted the reassurance. He would never again live with them. Not as he did now, as a dependent child, living with his parents. Maddening, exhausting his parents.

'Did you enjoy yourself last night?' This was the first time she'd raised the subject. He'd said he'd be home by one, but hadn't returned till after three. All she asked of him, when he changed his plans, was a phone call. Anytime, however late. He knew she worried. That she stayed awake, and grew frantic with worry. But he hadn't phoned. And what a state he must have been in, when he finally had got back. All that coughing and retching in the bathroom.

Alex grunted at her. Kay managed to hold her tongue. Never mind. It had been a last evening out with his friends. A last celebration before the eighteen-year-olds scattered like seedcorn across the country. The last time, maybe, he would make her suffer like that. Ah, the media would have you believe that it was girls you worried about, but ask any parent of teenagers; of course it was the boys. Boys: who got thumped for strolling the wrong streets, or looking at someone the wrong way. Who spiked each other's beers, and held spirit-drinking competitions. Who showed off behind their driving wheels, egged on by their raucous, reckless, tanked-up friends.

The wind dropped. They had rounded a headland. On the skyline now to their left were hummocks of old workings, their outlines softened with bilberry and heather. Alex nodded at them and said, 'You used to tell us that trolls lived over there.'

'As indeed they do.' Alex was going a long way back. Digging up memories. Nostalgic already.

'And that underneath, King Arthur slept in his cave. With all his warriors.'

'And don't forget the dragon.'

'Oh yeah. On its pile of gold.'

'Any myth you like. On your very doorstep.'

Alex halted. Impulsively he flung himself down on to the heather. The sun was hot here, out of the wind. A strong, yellow, late-September sun.

He rolled onto his stomach, so his face was half buried in the heather. 'Laura won't be coming over to Essex with Dad and me tomorrow. She told me last night.'

'Oh?' Kay found a dry flat stone and perched herself on it.

Alex turned his face to her. His expression was strained. 'She thinks … we ought to cool things. With, you know. Her in York, and me …'

He looked back at the heather. Kay sighed. A big soft motherly organ opened within her, and hurt for him. How dare Laura. Even if the girl didn't love him – as she clearly didn't – and might be right to do this, if she didn't.

'I'm so sorry,' she said. She knew Alex thought he loved Laura. Poor Alex. Such a romantic, emotional, whole-hearted boy.

Alex said, 'Yeah,' and sighed too, then screwed his eyes up. 'I suppose when I get to Essex they'll expect me to play rugby, shag sheep, and say boyo a lot. Shit.'

Kay smiled. 'Will you expect all the local girls to be called Sharon and wear white stilettos?'

'Ha ha.'

'Well then. It's the same for everyone.'

'I suppose I feel Welsh.'

'You can be Welsh, English, anything you like.'

Alex swivelled to face her. 'What was it like for you and Dad then? When you came here first? Being English. Didn't you feel kind of alien?'

Kay shook her head. 'Didn't cross our minds.' She laughed. 'The English don't think about being English. Like men don't think about maleness, or white people about whiteness. It was just an adventure.'

She brushed her hand over a particularly dense, springy clump of heather, pushing at its resilience. 'D'you remember that story? About the farmer who sat up here to smoke his pipe? Put his baccy down and it fell into what he thought was a rabbit hole. But he couldn't reach it, so he went home and got a torch. And when he shone it into the hole he saw that he was looking down into a vast chamber, a cathedral cave hollowed out in the limestone.'

Alex was silent. Then said, 'Why d'you tell me that?' and turned onto his back. He closed his eyes.

The words *we must protect the children* flickered across Kay's mind. But we mustn't baby them either, she thought. Why had that story occurred to her? Just after she had refused to identify with his sense that he was moving to a foreign land. Was she being cruel? Telling him a story that suggested that even the ground beneath his feet, the ground of his homeland, might not be solid or safe.

'I suppose,' said Alex, sighing, 'That it'll be weird for you too, now, with only Dad in the house.'

'Oh,' said Kay lightly. 'Women thrive on empty nests. We take up Open University courses and toy boys.'

Alex frowned at her.

Kay sighed. 'I don't expect much will change.' She wondered why she felt so flippant. Because, underneath, she was still angry with him, she supposed. Because she could face, quite easily today, the idea of life here without him.

Alex's profile tipped to the sky. 'This is kind of the end, though, isn't it?'

'The beginning, darling,' Kay corrected him. 'Surely.'

Alex exhaled a slow, punctured sigh. 'I'm gonna really miss Laura.'

'I am sorry.'

'That's why I got so drunk. Sorry if I woke you.'

'I wasn't asleep. You know me. I'm never asleep.' God, she thought wearily. But I will be now. He's leaving. From tomorrow, I shall sleep.

Alex half-smiled. 'I should really be up here with Dad, you know. Not you.'

'Should you?'

'It's traditional. You read about it. Dad and son take a walk in the hills, the day before son leaves for England. Mooch around together.'

'Do a spot of bonding?'

'Something like that.'

'You can do it tomorrow. On the drive over.'

'Yeah.' Alex's voice had a thin, insecure edge to it.

Oh dear, Kay thought. He's scared. But only a weak compassion stirred in her. A small, duty ache. And it dimmed beside another, much less charitable emotion, with a self-righteous voice that hissed: so it's your turn now, Alex, out there on your own. Now you'll start to understand.

She looked at her watch; it was past one o'clock. And it was still a fair walk back to the car. She got up.

Alex said, with his arm across his eyes, 'I don't want any lunch. I'll walk home.'

She frowned down at him. 'It'll take you hours.'

'I feel like it,' said Alex. 'Honestly.'

Kay shrugged. 'If you're sure.'

'Yeah.' Alex nodded. 'I am.'


Kay returned to the mountain car park for the car and drove home.

'Alex is walking back,' she told her husband Ed, who was laying the table in the kitchen. 'Says he feels like it. He's hung-over and miserable. Laura won't be going with you tomorrow, by the way. She dumped him last night.'

Ed's face twisted. 'Dumped him?'

'Yes. Bit cruel, I thought, doing it on his last day.'

Ed groaned, and then said, 'Maybe better than a Dear John letter in a few weeks. You can feel pretty low, in that first term.'

Kay realized he was right. She sighed. 'I think maybe you should have gone on the walk with him. He's scared. I couldn't seem to connect with it. I think I just made him worse.'

They had a soup and cheese lunch. She kept some back for Alex's return – not till about four, she guessed – then went outside to garden.


At five she returned to the kitchen and stared at the cooker clock. It said the same as her wrist-watch had outside. She found Ed, who was kneeling on the back seat of his car in the drive, rewiring the stereo speakers.

'Is Alex back?' she asked.

'Haven't seen him.'

'Right.' Kay went back into the house and upstairs to the landing. She opened Alex's bedroom door. On the carpet in the middle of the room was a pile of cardboard boxes, a portable CD player, an electric kettle, and an open, nearly full suitcase.

She nodded to herself. It was the beginning of something. She went downstairs, and back outside.

She built a bonfire at the bottom of the lawn. The wigwam of dry sticks caught immediately. When the flames were well-established she fed them with small logs, and then tossed on a wheelbarrow-load of perennial weeds. The fire pumped out thick grey smoke. Or was it steam? Whatever, it was smoke-signal stuff. She pulled a sour face at it. A home fire, burning.

A capricious gust of wind blew the dense grey plume into her face. Definitely smoke. Eyes streaming, she jabbed the pitchfork into the ground and stumbled back to the garden path. She almost bumped into Ed.

'No Alex yet?' She blotted her eyes with her sleeve.

Ed shook his head. She followed him into the kitchen. She didn't want to look at the clock, because clock-watching never produced missing children, but couldn't help herself. Nearly six. Ed was looking at her oddly.

'I got a faceful of smoke,' she explained, trying to smile.

'Why don't you come with us tomorrow?' he said. 'There'll be plenty of room now.'

She shook her head. 'I don't think so.' Five hours in a heavily laden car, in the back seat, probably, for at least some of it … no. She'd seen the university already, at an Open Day.

'He'll be back,' Ed said.

Kay wasn't sure if he meant this afternoon, or from Colchester.

'I know,' she murmured.

Ed turned to wash his hands in the sink. Kay felt her heart

start to thud, a slow, building drumbeat. A familiar tattoo. Oh God, she thought, last night was meant to be the end of this. Is he punishing me, for thinking that, and welcoming it? Do I have to go through this again?

'I can't start supper until he's back,' she said. 'Where the hell is he?'

'Alex is hopeless with time,' Ed said soothingly. 'You know he is.'

'Yes. But I wish Laura hadn't …' Now the subject was broached, her fear was rising. 'He's so emotional … and impulsive …'

'And selfish and unthinking,' said Ed. 'And not a hysteric. He's fine, you know he is.'

Did she? She saw Alex's face, pale and tragic. His arm, flung across his eyes. Heard his thin boy's voice crack. There were old quarries on the side of the mountain, with sheer unfenced cliffs. Further down, low-walled viaducts over deep gorges. Emotionally too, boys were more vulnerable than girls. The boy in the next street had cut his wrists when his girlfriend dumped him. Had stood in a phone box crying his grief to her, bleeding his life away, until he passed out. It was only luck that he had been found, and saved. And he hadn't had the prospect of leaving home the next day, of having to start a new life somewhere foreign and frightening, on top of his grief.

She gave up and let panic overwhelm her, though she despised herself for it. But she would panic for him, experience the loathsome, exhausting feelings, one more time. She poured herself a whisky, refused to start the evening meal or do anything that might take her mind off her son's absence. Contemplated, as the slow seconds ticked by, at what moment she would ring the police. Or mountain rescue. Or Laura. Sunset was at seven. It would be torchlight black by eight. As usual, she managed to hold in her mind the two incompatible convictions: that something terrible had happened to her son – because why else wasn't he here? – and that it hadn't, but that unless she worried for him, it surely would. Because that was when disaster struck, when you pooh-poohed the risks, and let your defences down.

By seven she was vindictive with rage and anxiety. She couldn't sit, or stand still, or occupy a static space at all. She tried to infect Ed, unsuccessfully; his resistance, as usual, was high. He had slept at night all through his children's adolescence. He cared, he insisted, but didn't believe that worrying helped: to Kay, a cruel, infuriating view, suggesting that beliefs and superstitions were optional, that she could spare herself this ordeal, if she so chose.

But Ed did at least, today, acknowledge her anxiety. He looked concerned. He said, 'D'you want me to go and search for him?'

She said, 'Yes, I do. I do,' and burst into tears. And then made the silent admission, feeling forced into it by her invisible, reproachful, missing son: that yes, life without him would be a catastrophe. That she would miss him, terribly.

And while Ed was comforting her, and trying to put on a coat at the same time, they heard footsteps outside. And then a cough, unmistakeably Alex's.

# SLIDESHOW

Mrs McAllister opens the front door to us, tired welcome on her brave Scottish face. Ian lets go my hand. I feel deserted, and have to force myself to follow him inside.

We're here for … a kind of wake, I suppose. For Stewart, Mrs McAllister's son. He died three weeks ago, on a student expedition to South America.

The others are already here, in the plum-and-sepia sitting-room. Robert, the expedition leader and photo-grapher – he's known the family for years. And Kate, Mrs McAllister's daughter. And a fair, tense-jawed young woman who must be Robert's girlfriend.

Robert gets up awkwardly from his armchair. I saw him at the funeral, but the hollows beneath his cheek-bones still shock. He's been sorting through a box of slides on the coffee table. He shakes Ian's hand, in the formal, rather old-fashioned way he has, and nods at me politely. I've only met him a few times; I wonder if he really wants me here.

Kate smiles up at me. Dear Kate. That's what I think, though I hardly know her, either. Exhaustion has ravaged her dark handsome face. She looks thirty-five, not twenty-five. She says, as if she means it, 'I'm so glad you've come.'

I smile back and murmur, 'Of course we've come.' What

I really want to say is, 'But I feel an intruder,' or 'I can't think why your mother suggested this,' because Kate's face invites confidences, but I can't; Stewart was her brother as well as Mrs McAllister's son, and I didn't know him well enough to grieve for him, and that makes me feel insecure. Ian is already talking easily to Robert and his girlfriend, but he was Stewart's best friend, and doesn't have to think about how to react.

Mrs McAllister wheels in a cane trolley with buttered scones and teacups. We had tea in the dining room, last time I was here, but maybe that's where they've set up the slide projector.

Robert's girlfriend jumps to her feet and says, 'Let me help you with that.'

'That's kind of you, Sandy.' Mrs McAllister picks up the plate of scones. 'Perhaps you'd pass these round.'

Sandy's eagerness makes me wonder how well she knew Stewart; maybe I'm not the only outsider.

As Mrs McAllister pours the tea she looks across to Robert. 'I hope you'll thank the others for coming down last week,' she says. 'We did appreciate it.'

Robert takes a scone from Sandy and says, much as I said to Kate, 'They wanted to be there. Naturally.'

They're talking about the funeral. And Alec and Richard, the other members of the expedition. Alec was still on crutches from his broken foot, and everyone was in awe of Richard, because of what he'd done. Kate and Robert were very protective of him. It made me realize, seeing the gentle way they treated him, how heroes might be victims too.

While Mrs McAllister is out of the room refilling the teapot Robert says quietly, 'I'll just show the ones up from the village.' He checks with Kate. 'Is that OK?'

She nods. 'As long as everyone's in them. And we can see where it happened. You know.'

She says it so matter-of-factly that I begin to relax. I tell myself that Mrs McAllister wouldn't have invited me here if she hadn't wanted me. Maybe outsiders serve a purpose. Maybe it'll lower the tension, something like that.

Robert rises. 'I'll go and set up.' He's only eaten half his scone.

'I'll give you a hand.' Ian pushes himself to his feet. Before they reach the doorway Mrs McAllister returns.

'Oh take the glasses through, Ian,' she says, setting the teapot down. 'You know where they are. The whisky's on the sideboard. We'll have a tot, afterwards.'

While the men are out of the room Kate asks Sandy how Robert is now.

Sandy's eyes flicker towards Mrs McAllister, as if she'd be happier to answer if she weren't here. I'm not sure why, because Kate's bereaved too, but I understand it. She gives a small shrug. 'Well … of course he still feels awful … and he misses Stewart dreadfully.' A straight courageous look at Mrs McAllister, followed by a wan smile at me, acknowledgement that Ian must be feeling much the same. She sighs. 'But in himself, he's a lot better. He's putting on weight now.'

Robert had dysentery in Lima. That's why he went only as far as camp two, because he was still weak and he'd have been a liability on the ascent. It's lucky he was out of it; if he'd been injured or killed Richard couldn't possibly have coped.

Kate turns to her mother. 'Robert's just going to show the shots up from the village. I've said that's fine. He'll give us prints of the rest.'

Mrs McAllister nods and puts her cup and saucer down with a rattle. There's an uncomfortable silence before she rises abruptly and says, 'I'm sure they must be ready for us.'

In the dining room the heavy velvet curtains are drawn. The projector rests on a stack of leather-bound books at the

end of the dining table. There's no screen; two antique maps
have been removed from the far wall.

Mrs McAllister and Kate sit on Robert's left; Ian, Sandy
and I on his right. I touch Ian's arm as I sit down but it
doesn't register; he looks distant and preoccupied. Sandy
keeps tucking her fair hair behind her ears, even though it's
already there. Her eyes are permanently on Robert. Robert
switches the projector on and a large white rectangle appears
on the end wall.

'I'll do the lights, shall I?' I say, pushing my chair back. I'm
grateful for something to do; like Sandy, I guess, with the
scones. I stand by the switch waiting for Robert's signal.
He nods.

The first slide is a dazzle of colours and light. As I slip
back into my chair the picture resolves itself. It's a crowd
of exotic strangers: men, women and children, black-
haired and grinning, wearing hats and capes and skirts in
brilliant, geometrically-patterned primary colours. I think
immediately of Aztecs, or Incas. Behind them, unnatural-
looking and jarring, are slivers of fluorescent orange tent.
The top quarter of the shot is deep blue sky. I search the
picture but there's no Stewart here, no one I recognize. I
consciously loosen my shoulders.

'These are the villagers at base camp,' Robert says.
'Stunning, aren't they? The women make all the clothes
themselves. Spin the wool, dye it, weave it, the lot. It's so
remote that they have to be completely self-sufficient.'

Kate's voice says, 'It looks cold.'

'Only at night,' says Robert. 'It's hot midday. It's summer
there, of course.'

The next slide comes up. This is it. The four of them, a
posed group shot. They're standing beneath a cloth banner
which reads 'Strathclyde Geographical Club'. Richard and
Robert at either side, Stewart and Alec between them.

Stewart is looking straight at camera, grinning, one foot raised and resting, mighty-hunterlike, on a bulging rucksack. Invisible wind is pressing curls of black hair across his forehead. Robert, to his right, looks out at us gaunt-faced but smiling. In his hand is a small gadget which must be the remote camera control. Alec's cheerful round face is caught with his mouth in a goldfish O. Richard alone seems to have missed Robert's cue; his grin is directed not at camera, but sideways, across the others.

In the room no one says anything. There's a gaiety in the shot that's numbing. It's the wrong picture; we're the wrong audience. I can't look at Stewart. My gaze rests on Richard, the only one who isn't looking back. His features are open and uncomplicated, like those of so many large strong men. Innocent, almost.

That's what's wrong with the picture: its terrible innocence.

Then a click; before us are huge, empty mountains. Beside me Ian clears his throat. We all shift in our seats. Robert says, in a normal, neutral voice. 'This is from just above the village.' At the edge of my vision I'm aware of his lifting arm. 'It's the one in the middle.'

I'm surprised. My eyes were on a snow-capped peak to the left, a dangerous-looking mountain with sheer, knife-edged scalloped sides. The middle peak is much lower, snowless and grey-green, its shoulders round and benign-looking. Even to me, it looks conquerable. I remind myself that this was a geographical, not a mountaineering, expedition. They weren't meant to be testing themselves.

'But they look so close,' Mrs McAllister says. It sounds almost a complaint. 'Is this really from the village?'

'Just above,' says Robert. 'It's the huge scale of things out there. And the air's so thin, there's very little distance haze. It was a ten-hour walk to camp one, and another eight to camp two, just below the shale.'

He says *the shale* without hesitation or emphasis, but it's still like receiving an electric shock. Stewart was killed on the shale. Robert is pitching us forwards. I see a flash of forbidden image: a picture that exists somewhere in my mind, but which I refuse to look at. Especially in front of Mrs McAllister and Kate.

Now come slides of the walk from base camp to camp one. Three laden figures, bare-armed and hatless, dwarfed by the vastness of a moss-green treeless landscape. The figures, you feel, are there only to give scale to the rest. In most I can distinguish only Richard, because of his size.

But a close shot now, of Alec, Stewart and Richard, squatting round a lavender-like shrub. Alec, the botanist, is cutting off a small sprig. Stewart's head is tilted to Richard, who is unscrewing a canister, frowning down into it with concentration. All seem unaware of Robert and the camera. The picture is a record of the shrub – it's centre frame, a sharp-focused, unimpeded view – and at the same time a picture of men working: visible proof – and to me, after the gaiety of that first group shot, it urgently needs proving – that Stewart died not on a frivolous, unnecessary holiday, but at work. My heart, which had started to thud as the figures appeared, calms again with relief.

Another click, and we're at what must be camp one. Two orange tents side by side, a heap of multi-coloured rucksacks on the green sward between them. Rising directly behind the tents is the dull grey-green mass of the round-shouldered mountain. Someone in a blue anorak – Alec, I think – is on the right of the picture, bent over a stove. The light suggests that it's evening, and the hunch of Alec's shoulders that it's cold.

'Which day is this?' Kate's voice asks. 'Was it one night here, or two?'

'Just the one,' says Robert. 'We only planned four nights away from the village. Two out, two back.'

I can't remember now how long they were gone. I've been told, but the details don't stick. It's because of that terrible image. My mind sheers away.

'Why didn't they come looking for you?' Mrs McAllister asks. 'Surely, when you were late … ?'

In the gloom Robert hesitates before replying. I sense he wants to say, tactfully, that this isn't the Cairngorms, that there are are no telephones to call up mountain rescue or helicopters, that the villagers wouldn't necessarily see a party of young westerners as their responsibility.

'We were only a day and a half late,' he says finally. 'The weather was good, it's not a difficult climb. They'd no reason to suppose anything was wrong.'

I remember now: only one extra night. How long would it have been, if they had waited for help? It was a two-day walk from the village, for able-bodied men. A five day round trip. Suppose the villagers had given them, what, six days? Stewart would already have been dead four. Another two before they were reached. Alec with a broken foot. Perhaps Richard should have left the others, run down for help. He could have been back in three, four, days. Would I leave a friend, even if he were fit and strong, which Robert wasn't, to care for an injured man and a dead body, for three days?

It is as if the next slide is flooding straight from my mind. It's a close shot of a rock outcrop, but in effect, because he is standing foreground, a portrait of Richard. He's side view to us, a small thin-handled hammer in his right hand. We must be well above camp one here, because on the left of the picture, where we can see beyond the outcrop, the green sward had given way to lichen-stained boulders and tufts of coarse vegetation.

Robert says that this is just below camp two. I scarcely hear him. I am still with Richard, in those desperate crisis hours. Should he and Robert have buried Stewart? Made a cairn over him? Collected him later, with the villagers? How long can you leave a body, in the ground or above, and hope to recover it? What responsibility do you feel to a dead friend? Or to his mother, and sister?

I am staring at Richard's shoulders. Shoulders broad and strong enough to carry a man. I can think it, just, without seeing it. Did he know he could do it? So in fact have no choice? Was he truly victim, rather than hero? Fated to carry the dead body of a friend, for three days, simply because he could?

He couldn't have known. No one could know that.

My eyes travel down Richard's arms to his hands, which must have lifted Stewart's body – how many times, over the three days? – adjusted, steadied, held him.

The image swamps me. I can't hold it back. Oh God, how can Kate and her mother bear this? The terrible, treacherous image: their brother, son, pathetic dead-weight baggage …

But suddenly here is Stewart. Alive. My mind is wiped clear. We are at camp two. He is in half-profile, a day's stubble on his chin, bareheaded, expression serious, very handsome. From a leather belt slung cowboy-style round his hips hang the tools of his geologist's trade. He looks both professional and romantic.

Robert says, 'I thought you might like a blow-up of this. It's the last of Stewart, on his own.'

Kate's voice, low and husky, says, 'It's wonderful.' I glance across at her. Her eyes are luminous with tears.

Mrs McAllister tugs a handkerchief from her sleeve and blows her nose ferociously. Her voice when she speaks is tremulous, not with grief, but with pride.

'He was a fine boy.' Fiercely she shakes her head. 'A fine boy.'

I look back up at Stewart, and agree. Sandy's face is tipped up to the image too, her lips apart, eyes pale with reflected light.

Suddenly I know why I'm here. And Sandy. Suddenly I can see everything, without fear. There's nothing to be frightened of. Mrs McAllister's proud of her son. We're not intruders; she wants us all to see him, her beloved only son. She's not embarrassed by his death, or the manner of his death, or his undignified journey after death. Nor is Kate. Why should they be? It's just the truth. It's frightened only me, and maybe Sandy, the outsiders, who didn't love him.

'And this is the last one,' Robert is saying. 'The three of them, starting the ascent.'

As we gaze at the slide – three distant figures, yellow-helmeted, coils of rope across their bodies, but still walking, rather than climbing – Robert moves round the dining table. He stands to one side of the picture.

'The shale slip must have started here,' he says, pointing up the picture to what looks like the dark lower reaches of a vertical gash in the mountainside. His moving arm, as it crosses the image, is dappled with shifting translucent colours. 'Something gave, and the whole lot came down. Alec was here – ' he taps a spot below, to the right of the gully, ' – and Stewart here – ' his palm brushes the wall directly beneath it. 'They're actually on a track, though you can't see it.'

I ask, boldly, 'Where was Richard?'

'Above and a bit to the right of Alec,' says Robert, pointing. 'Well clear.'

Beside me Ian stirs, 'Any idea now, what caused it?'

Robert shrugs. 'Could have been a number of things. A goat, possibly, though it's a bit high. Water, tiny earth tremor, even wind.'

'Did you see it?' Kate asks. Before Robert can answer, Sandy asks, 'Have there been slips there before?' The atmosphere is changing. It's becoming animated, inquiring.

Robert says, to Sandy, 'No, it's considered a safe ascent.'

Then to Kate, 'I heard it, more than saw it. I was taking rock samples. I could see dust through the binoculars, but not much else. Then after a couple of minutes I saw Richard's flare. I went up and helped Alec down while he got Stewart.'

'Terrible,' says Mrs McAllister. Her voice is deep and thick, but strong. 'You poor boys.'

'Thank God for you and Richard,' sighs Kate. She says it so sincerely, so unselfishly, I want to embrace her. I reach for Ian's hand under the table; he responds this time, enfolding my fingers with his.

'What did you do with all the gear?' he asks. His hand on mine is warm, encouraging. 'The packs and tents. You had to leave them, I suppose?'

Robert says, 'Ah well …' scratching his ear. He pulls out a chair and sits down. We're into the nitty-gritty now, the air's filling with questions. Some, I realize, might even be mine. Above Robert's head the mountain and the yellow-capped figures shine out, icon-like, dominating the room. Before he can continue Mrs McAllister calls for drinks.

Ian passes round whiskies as Robert talks. Nobody turns the light on, or cuts the projector. The bottle is left in the middle of the table, within everyone's reach.

We listen to Robert. We ask questions, repeat answers, talk across each other. At one point Kate weeps, but unself-consciously, and it alters nothing. At another someone changes the slide on the wall for the beautiful one of Stewart, and Mrs McAllister challenges anyone to have a finer son.

We finish the bottle of whisky, and open another. And finally drink toasts, with unrestrained, fervent words, to everyone.

# IN MITIGATION

My Lord, thank you for allowing me this chance to speak in mitigation. I do appreciate being able to explain, from my point of view, the facts of the case.

To do this, however, My Lord, I have to tell you certain things about myself, and some, I'm afraid, are a little ... indelicate. I hope you will bear with me. It is all, I assure you, relevant. I will be as brief as possible.

I am, as you know, My Lord, a person of middle years – forty-five, to be exact – and I hold down, in my position as a Complaints Officer for British Gas, a responsible and stressful job. However, I am also a woman, and, like all women of child-bearing age, live my life according to a ... well, shall we say ... biological cycle.

My apologies. I can see that even those careful words have made some here instantly uncomfortable; but I regret that, to explain, I must go even further.

Since I ceased taking the contraceptive pill some years ago my ... biological cycle has shortened from the standard twenty-eight days to twenty-four. This is a common experience. The event itself lasts for six days, and, in recent years, has become more troublesome. Without being gruesome or tastelessly explicit, I would just say that the sensation, at least for three of the six days, is of being literally and metaphorically drained.

Oh dear. I see from faces before me that I am deep in unwelcome territory. I am sorry, My Lord, but what I describe is a tedious fact of life for a not insignificant section of the population, and we should, surely, be allowed to speak of it. It is also crucially relevant to this case.

So I will continue. Now, for three days before my period I experience, as many women do, an increase in internal tension. I become, I readily admit, more irritable and intolerant than usual. I also, for at least one night during these three days, experience muscular tension so severe as to render sleep impossible. This adds, not unnaturally, to my irritability the following day. The human rights organisation Amnesty, I would remind My Lord, regards sleep deprivation as a form of torture.

In addition to this, for the last five years I have also experienced – in common, again, with many women of my age – a second mid-cycle spell of tension. A pre-ovulatory tension. This lasts a couple of days. It mimics the premenstrual experience, except that it has a more anxious, anticipatory, frantic feel to it. It is, if anything, more unpleasant.

Ovulation itself, which was once a silent, undetectable event, is, these days – I am not alone here either – a matter of discomfort. Sometimes merely an hour or so of cramping twinges, but occasionally – if a drop of blood is expelled from the ovary at the same time, or a strand of endometrial material becomes involved – excruciatingly painful. The sort of pole-axing, white-knuckle persistent pain that, if experienced by any group other than middle-aged women, would, one feels sure, result in immediate hospitalization.

And this is not the end of it, My Lord. Once ovulation is over there are several days – up to four, maybe – of intense sexual tension. Biologically programmed into maturer women, possibly, to make the most of, and focus effort into, the small fertile windows of these last childbearing years.

During these sexually charged days my thoughts – if I didn't rigorously discipline them – would be constantly distracted.

I apologize once more; I am again embarrassing the court. But the point of what I am saying, My Lord, is I hope now clear. In each twenty-four day cycle there are at least fifteen days when, constitutionally, I am not at my best. Fifteen in every twenty-four when I have to contain my impulses, whether these be aggressive, sexual, or merely hibernatory. And I do contain them, My Lord. Despite the powerful internal pressures generated, I live an outwardly decorous, continent, and productive life.

So. In the light of what I have told you, let me describe what happened at Foster's Garage on the afternoon in question.

I arrived at the garage, as I'd arranged with Mr Foster over the telephone, at exactly three o'clock. I had explained to him already the urgency with which I needed my puncture repaired, and the fact that I had an important meeting some miles away at four.

When I arrived there was no one in the office, but I could hear voices in an adjacent workshop. I was sure that who-ever was talking must have heard my car arrive, and the slam of the office door, so I waited for a few minutes in the empty room. The voices I could hear very distinctly. They were, I recall, talking first about the National Lottery, and then about something or someone called the Horny Devils. These are, I now know, the local pub darts team.

At ten past three I became anxious. I left the office and walked round to the workshop, the big double doors of which were standing wide open. I could see two men, one small and greasy-looking in overalls, whom I took – correctly – to be Mr Foster. I positioned myself at the doors so I could be clearly seen, without trespassing into the work area, and tried to catch his eye. Mr Foster, however, though he was turned towards me and must have seen me, steadfastly refused to acknowledge my presence. He simply continued his conversation. On the wall behind him, I couldn't help but notice, were numerous pictures of naked and revoltingly posed young women. I felt, as I stood there trying and failing to catch his eye, successively invisible, intimidated, and foolish. And, finally, furious.

At twenty past three my patience expired. I walked up to Mr Foster, cut across his conversation, and said, 'Excuse me. I rang earlier about a puncture. I am in a hurry.' I may have spoken sharply, My Lord, but the words were no ruder than that.

Mr Foster, however, looked at me with affronted astonishment, as he might have looked if one of the nearby cars, rather than a human being, had rebuked him. Then he recovered himself. He shot a smirking smile at his friend and said, in as patronizing a tone as it is possible to imagine, 'Right lady. You drive in here then.' And as I turned to get the car I heard him say, in a stage whisper to his companion, 'Wrong time of the month for someone, eh?'

My Lord, I'm afraid I snapped. Given what I have just told you about myself, this remark seemed to me quite unacceptable. I would not have it. For someone, a man, who has never had a wrong time of the month in his life, to snidely demean – with no understanding of the suffering, self-discipline and control involved – someone who has, at least at present, more wrong than right days, was intolerable. He was showing no respect for the fact that he, and his children, and his children's children only exist, or will exist, because of women's bodies, and what, for the benefit of man and womankind, they endure. To men like Mr Foster, I suspect, women are non-people. Merely smut when they are young, and invisible or joke fodder as they grow older.

The irony is, My Lord, that that day at the garage was

not, for me, a wrong time of the month. I am not standing here asking for leniency because, that day, I was not myself. I was entirely myself. The incident occurred on one of the few days out of every twenty-four when I felt quite uninfluenced by hormonal stress. I do not, of course, even on influenced days, allow my actions to reflect my wilder feelings, but that is irrelevant here. I was, on the day in question, a rational but humiliated woman, provoked by this patronizing little man, beyond reason.

I never intended to run him down, though I know he believed otherwise. But I did, My Lord, intend to frighten him, and I was reckless, I accept, as to the consequences of my actions. However I was not aware that there was an inspection pit beyond him, into which a rapidly retreating person might fall. I regret that he was hurt and am glad he has made a full recovery. But I cannot accept that my actions were 'wilfully psychopathic' as the prosecution would have it, nor that the blame for the incident should be solely mine. Men like Mr Foster have to learn, My Lord. They have to learn how to behave. They have to learn what is offensive, and inflammatory, and unacceptable. And, in particular, My Lord, they have to understand that they should be very careful, at all times of every month, what they say to middle-aged women.

# LEARNING TO SPEAK KLINGON

The streets of the Valleys town are cold and blustery in January, but not unfriendly. The square in front of the cinema is even picturesque, in a downbeat, frontier-town way. It bears a passing resemblance, certainly after a few pints, to the fifties town square filmset in *Back to the Future*.

Up a side road is a row of tall, substantial brickbuilt houses and in one of these Iestyn and Dale, two young men in their early twenties, rent a large first floor flat. They have two bedrooms, big sitting-room, kitchen and bathroom, with gas central heating, all for £35 a week each. Which the DSS pays, as neither young man has a job. Neither, it should be said, is seriously looking for one: Iestyn is lead singer for a local heavy rock band called War Zone, a group much in demand, and Dale is taking A levels in Media Studies and Psychology at evening classes and doesn't want to overstretch himself. Both young men are, anyway, of the opinion that in the present economic climate, with not enough work to go round, it would be positively selfish of them to hog jobs they don't want, when there are others clearly desperate for them.

Both young men's weeks, despite their unemployed status, are full. They rise about noon. During the afternoon they do chores such as shopping or tidying up or going to the launderette or signing on, and Iestyn walks his dog

Duffy, which he isn't meant to keep at the flat but which
the landlord has given up nagging him about. Iestyn is a
young man of infectious good humour and even the landlord is susceptible. While he's out Dale does any college
homework he's been set. Both drop in on parents, sisters or
aunties for tea, or treat themselves at the chippie, and then
the day's real business begins. For Iestyn, Tuesday and Sunday are band practice nights – held in a nearby disused
chapel – and most Fridays and Saturdays the band has gigs.
As far away as Swansea, sometimes. The money they make
covers their expenses. On Monday nights he has a regular
spot at the Bridgend pub down the road, compèring their
karaoke evenings, singing himself, in his confident, rock-
singer's voice, if no one else will take the microphone.
Despite – or perhaps because of – his Red-Indian length hair,
earrings and tattoos, he is a favourite with the regulars,
especially the women. The pub manager pays him in Pilsner
beer and a tenner in cash.

Dale's evenings are almost as busy: he has his classes
Tuesdays and Thursdays, seven until ten, and roadies for
Iestyn when the band has gigs. Wednesday night both young
men make sure they are home early evening for *Star Trek*.
Dale is a model-maker as well as a *Star Trek* enthusiast and
his bedroom is ornamented with neat rows of Federation
Enterprises, Klingon Birds of Prey, Ferengi Marauders and
Romulan Warbirds. After the programme he is often inspired
to start a new model. And this January he has begun teach-
ing himself the Klingon language, from a Star Trek dictionary given to him at Christmas by his mother. He's tried to
persuade Iestyn to learn too, but with only limited success.
'It's a warrior language, mun,' he's insisted, thinking this
will appeal to the hard man of rock in Iestyn. Klingons, with
their long hair and macho dress, look very Heavy Metal.
'The language of brutal reality,' he stresses. 'Genuine fighting

talk. And half as many people in the world speak Klingon as speak Welsh, you know.'

'Not in Wales, they don't,' Iestyn points out. But he has deigned to learn the odd word. *NuqneH*, for instance, pronounced *nook-NEKH*, which translated means *what do you want?* the nearest the barbaric language gets to *hello*. And *Qo*, pronounced *kkho*, which means *I won't*.

So: Iestyn with his music, and Dale with his hobbies and studies, enjoy busy, relatively fulfilled lives. Which doesn't seem to be the case for their neighbours.

Below Iestyn and Dale, in the smaller, darker, ground floor flat, live a young couple and their baby, Pete, Mouse, and Baby Mouse. (Dale and Iestyn have never been told the child's proper name.) Pete is unemployed too and not a great conversationalist. Iestyn and Dale feel that Pete is the sort of unemployed bloke that they'd like their non-participation in the labour market to benefit, because he clearly needs a job, and isn't good at managing without one. He doesn't seem to have any hobbies or enthusiasms or inner resources at all. He always looks miserable, always at a loose end. Trouble is, he's also the sort of guy who doesn't get jobs. Who's the last to hear about the few there are. Doesn't put himself about. You have to hustle for jobs these days. The quiet, passive types don't stand a chance. 'He's dull, too, man,' Dale says with a sigh. 'No two ways about it.'

Mouse, however, is not dull. They actually see more of her than Pete because the baby often has colic and colds and she comes upstairs to ring the surgery from their phone. (Rock bands have to be bookable; group funds pay the rental.) Mouse is tiny, as her name suggests, and would be pretty if she didn't look permanently tired. Iestyn thinks it's a miracle that a body as small as hers carried and gave birth to a baby. Baby Mouse is fat and cute – more hamster than mouse, really – despite the colic and colds.

In February the manager of the Bridgend asks Iestyn if he'd like to work behind the bar Wednesday and Thursday evenings. Iestyn says no, ta, his diary's already full, but he'll find someone else, leave it to him. He sees a chance to do Pete and Mouse a favour. He tells Mouse, who tells Pete, who is told again, impatiently, by Iestyn, and finally it's fixed. Pete will work eight till twelve both evenings for twenty quid a week.

There's only one problem: Mouse, though she wants the extra money and thinks the work'll do Pete good, doesn't like being left alone in the flat at night. It's on the ground floor, and the back kitchen doesn't have curtains. They've had one attempted break-in already. The garden outside spooks her. Anyone might be looking in. She tells Dale and Iestyn, who invite her and the baby upstairs on the nights that Pete's out. The baby is tucked up on the big sofa, Duffy warned not to slobber on him, and on Wednesdays Mouse watches Dale build models and Iestyn sketch War Zone flyers and CD covers. Dale practises his Klingon on her too. *Hijol!* he says, which means *Beam me aboard*. Or *bImoHqu* which means *you look terrible*. Most Klingon phrases are negative or aggressive and require a back-of-throat explosive delivery; it's the brutal Klingon way. Mouse has a sense of humour. While Dale is trying a longer phrase on her she inquires if he's being sick. 'That means surrender or die,' Dale tells her. 'Ah, useful,' Mouse nods.

On Thursday nights when she goes upstairs Mouse has Iestyn to herself until ten-thirty, because it's a college night for Dale. Normally Iestyn would go out, just for a quick pint and perhaps a video to watch later with Dale, but he's only going out for company, and if company's coming upstairs, he's happy to stay in. Mouse has very neat handwriting and helps Iestyn copy out lyric and order-of-play sheets for the band. He discovers that she and Pete have family down the valley that they don't see much of, because there was bad feeling about the baby. Pete used to have a good job when they lived down there, but the firm went bust and he didn't even get redundancy. She says Pete worries a lot and used to be more fun. She says it apologetically and even a touch flirtatiously, suggesting that she still likes a bit of fun. And maybe likes Iestyn too. Iestyn can flirt with the best of them and knows how automatic it is in the company of anyone half-way attractive – which he knows he is – so doesn't take it seriously. He has sex regularly enough with girls he meets at gigs not to want to complicate life at home. And although he likes Mouse, he knows that any attachment they made wouldn't last. A rock singer's life is too promiscuous. So, for Mouse's sake, he makes no move on her.

But Pete starts to get paranoid about the arrangement anyway. He says he didn't realize Dale was out Thursdays, and he's not sure now he wants Mouse upstairs alone with Iestyn. People talk about Iestyn in the pub; how the women try to touch him up when he sings *I'm Too Sexy* on the karaoke, and how he wiggles his bum and encourages them.

Pete and Mouse row about it one night. Mouse has a very loud voice for someone so small. From upstairs Iestyn and Dale can hear her shouting, 'You think', 'You think', 'You think', over and over again. Finally the baby starts screaming, which shuts them up. Dale says to leave them be, but Iestyn's restless – you could kill Mouse with one punch, he thinks – and goes down and knocks on their door. Pete opens it and says, 'And you can fuck off, too,' and slams it shut again. But Iestyn has heard Mouse snap, 'For God's sake, Pete,' from somewhere inside the flat and is reassured, so he doesn't knock again.

Mouse tells Iestyn when they pass in the hallway the next day that she won't be coming up again. He tries to help her with the pushchair over the front steps but she says, 'Leave it. I can manage.' She sounds angry, and tired.

Then, next thing they know, Pete has given up the pub job. And the manager is cross; he tells Iestyn they've had the DSS in, checking up on workers. Iestyn's annoyed, because of his own position, and pissed off with Pete, for getting caught out on a job he organized for him.

Next time he sees Mouse, on the street outside with the baby, he asks what's going on. Mouse's chin stiffens and she shakes her head and says, 'It's not fair. It's always us.'

'What is?' Iestyn asks.

Mouse sighs and invites him in for coffee. Pete is out. Mouse puts the baby in the cot in the front bedsitting room and boils the kettle for Iestyn in the kitchen. 'They've stopped his money,' she tells him. 'Because he was working.'

Iestyn asks how they found out, but Mouse has no idea. Iestyn reckons Pete gives off guilty vibes. He's met this before; it's always the honest ones, the ones who really want jobs, who hate being on the dole, who get investigated. They get asked if they've worked, and they can't lie convincingly. It's like the teacher's end-of-tether punishment that always falls on the one kid who doesn't deserve it. The DSS never touch people like himself, people who can pull strokes with confidence. They hit men who are already down; the easy targets.

Mouse says they haven't stopped her or the baby's money and they'll maybe start Pete's again in April when they've finished their investigation and he's paid back what he owes. 'But it's made him really low,' she says. 'He's not sleeping. And he doesn't talk. Except to keep saying that he's gotta get a job.' She pauses, and then says, with her jaw grim as if it's a hard thing for her to say, 'He doesn't do much about it, though. I'm going right off him. He's a loser, I tell you.'

This is no news to Iestyn. Iestyn knows that these days you've got to use the system, or buck it, and be tough about it. Decide what you want, for you, and go for it. You've got to have energy, drive, purpose. Pete can't hack it. He's waiting for someone else to help him, the system to work for him, and it won't happen. It's a jungle out there; jungle laws apply.

Thinking about Pete makes Iestyn angry. With Pete. It's as if Pete's a reminder he doesn't want. He suddenly feels a desire to hurt Pete himself, for being so helpless, for being a loser.

Mouse is looking very small and vulnerable and it's easy to put his arms around her. She responds as if she hasn't had her hands on a man, her body against a man's body, since Baby Mouse was conceived. Iestyn can almost convince himself he's doing her a favour. They don't want to disturb the baby so they move to the big plastic-covered bench the dining end of the kitchen. Iestyn can be an unselfish lover when he puts his mind to it, and he particularly wants to give Mouse a good time; by the end her small naked body is tacky with sweat, her arms and legs squeaking as they jerk against the plastic, and she is making faint glutted noises in her throat. Iestyn pulls her up from the bench – she weighs nothing – and cuddles her, and she cries a little, but smiles at him too. Iestyn knows that sex can make people happy and sad at the same time, though he doesn't feel anything himself now, at all; satisfying her seems to have emptied him.

He doesn't tell Dale what has happened. Dale would disapprove. Dale's got a girlfriend himself at the moment, a seventeen-year-old schoolgirl who doesn't laugh at his spaceships and who has learnt *My engine is overheating* and *Does it bite?* in Klingon.

Nor does Iestyn repeat the experience with Mouse. He makes no decision about this; the opportunity simply doesn't arise. Pete seems to be home all the time. Iestyn sees Mouse taking Baby Mouse out to the park, and sometimes he thinks about following her, but what would be the point?

He admits that he now actively dislikes Pete. This is rare; there aren't many people Iestyn dislikes. But seeing Pete screws his guts up into a tight fist. He tried to help Pete, and Pete fouled things up. And made him feel responsible. He resents that. He thinks of Mouse sharing that dark dismal flat with Pete, eating with him, sleeping with him. Having sex with him, maybe. Bring dragged down by him.

Then one Monday in April, late afternoon, there's a knock on the door. Dale answers it and it's Mouse, in a coat and carrying Baby Mouse, also swaddled up for outdoors. She says hello, Dale, Iestyn; long time no see. There's a taxi outside – she's going back to her Mum's. Just wants them to know, in case anyone asks after her. She gives them an address and phone number. Iestyn wonders if she's trying to give them to him but can't tell – or ask – with Dale there. He can't imagine wanting to use them, anyway. He had sex last weekend with a girl built like an Amazon who licked her finger and notched him up on her bedstead afterwards. Not the sort who wept over him. He's glad Mouse is going, for her sake, and his own. He wonders what Pete'll do now.

It doesn't take long to find out. Nine days later the police come round. Pete has fallen – or jumped – off one of the disused railway viaducts at the edge of town, and he's dead. Dale and Iestyn go round the dark downstairs flat with the policemen, to see if Pete's left a note, but he hasn't. Just a pile of dirty dishes in the kitchen sink. The bed in the bed-sitting room is unmade and the bottom sheet is grey. The bathroom and toilet are filthy. Iestyn remembers Mouse's skinny naked body splayed across the plastic-covered kitchen bench and is relieved she got away. He reckons Pete would have done this anyway – at least he didn't take anyone else with him. He tells the police the guy was out of work and always miserable and he's not surprised he wanted out. Maybe it's even for the best. He gives them Mouse's address and phone number, and says she'll know where Pete's parents live.

Then he and Dale go back upstairs. It's Wednesday evening and as usual they watch *Star Trek*. Iestyn can tell from the way Dale stares at the screen trying not to blink that he's upset by Pete's death; so afterwards, to take his friend's mind off things, he encourages him to paint one of his models and offers to test him on his Klingon phrases. Looking at the Useful Klingon Expressions section of the dictionary he gets Dale to say the Klingon for *That is unfortunate* and *It's not my fault*. And, eventually, though it's a long difficult sentence, he gets Dale to master the quintessential Klingon life-is-cheap saying: *Four thousand throats may be cut in one night, by a running man*.

# A HOLIDAY ROMANCE

Surviving the air flight had a profound effect on Helen. Great fear sends little fears, like tiny spiders in the face of a monstrous bird-eating relative, scuttling for the cracks. She had survived; life could threaten no worse terrors. Her flight companions, stepping onto the scorching concrete of Zakynthos Town runway, gasped and seemed to physically wilt in the afternoon heat. Helen inhaled the same air, enjoyed the sensation of her body greeting it, a million skin pores opening and moistening in welcome, and thought she had never felt more fear-free, more triumphantly euphoric, in her life.

An hour later, dropped off at her apartment by the Summer Sun Tour coach, she strolled across the dark tiled bedroom floor, still feeling brave and confident. She threw open the balcony shutters, letting light pour into the room; and the air outside rushed in too, with a silent roar, enveloping her in heat. She turned to study the plain, underfurnished room and to decide which of the two neat white-sheeted beds would be hers, and which would be her friend Margaret's, when she arrived next week. Their staggered arrival dates were a result of Margaret's father's death a week ago. At Margaret and Helen's ages, parental deaths were an all-too-common occurrence. Both Helen's own parents had died the previous year, the year she turned fifty. They, too, had chosen

131

inconvenient times: one just before her brother's second
marriage celebrations, the other on Christmas Eve.

Helen took off all her clothes and showered in the tiny
windowless bathroom. There was no shower curtain, only
a hand-held nozzle, and nowhere to hang a towel; but Helen
had read her Greek Island Tour guide, and expected no
better. At least there was water pressure. At least the light
worked. She walked, naked and dripping, from the bathroom to the bedroom and could feel, just in those few
seconds, hot air suck the moisture from her skin.

There was no long mirror in the room. No danger of catch-
ing sight of herself. She felt good – middle-aged flesh, experienced from within, definitely blossomed in heat. She lay
down on the bed she had chosen for herself and closed her
eyes. Her life in Britain, her flat in Bristol, the primary
school where she was headmistress, her friends, colleagues,
relatives, seemed more than a few countries away. They
belonged to a distant, diminishing, suddenly dismissable
life. She remembered the Valium she'd taken that the doctor
had given her for the flight, which hadn't killed the fear but
had, presumably, muted her body's reaction to it. She felt
now extraordinarily relaxed.

Sleepily she spread her arms wide, so they hung in space,
either side of the bed. She was a starfish, adrift and abandoned
on a white undiscovered beach. She could not remember
when she had last savoured a moment so intensely.

When she woke the light outside was beginning to fail.
Dusk, she guessed, would be a brief event in Greece. She
could hear voices and laughter. Young, male, English voices.
She smiled; excited voices. It must be the four young men
who had been shown by the tour guide into the corner apartment next door. Their balcony adjoined hers. One of them,
a fluffy-looking boy, surely no older than twenty, had
reminded her of her sister's son.

She rose, wrapped the sheet around herself, and stood in the doorway to the balcony. The sea, edged in tiny lulling waves, was still a glittering, kingfisher blue. About half a mile out a small green and brown island rose like a crusted gemstone from the waters. A protected, turtle-nesting island, they'd been told on the coach. In the courtyard below the balcony, bordering the beach road, was a line of trees with grey-green, feathery, asparagus-like foliage which lifted and dipped in the light evening breeze. 'Beautiful, beautiful,' Helen's lips murmured.

She leant forward to look along the beach road. She had imagined, when Margaret told her that she would miss the first week, that meals would be difficult. That she would end up cooking for herself in the apartment kitchenette, because she wouldn't want to eat out alone. But now, here, and in this new euphoric mood, the idea seemed ridiculous. She could see a taverna not fifty yards away; the coloured lights were already on, soft Greek music already playing. The smell of meat cooking on a charcoal grill made saliva spring to her mouth. She was ravenous.

She unpacked quickly, selected a sleeveless cotton dress and slipped it on. And tonight, because as yet she had no tan, applied foundation, lipstick, and eye make-up.

Outside on the stairs she was overtaken by the four boys from the corner apartment: a small pounding herd of young masculinity. A little drunk already, she suspected. Well, why not. They managed to avoid trampling her to the concrete without actually appearing to notice her. Helen was used to being invisible to young men. They wore jeans and white T-shirts with bold legends, and when they reached the beach road galloped away from her and the taverna; making for Laganas town, she guessed, round the headland, with its all-night discos and bars. And girls.

She strolled on to the taverna. Two families were already

seated beneath the rush canopy. Helen found herself a small table and firmly caught a young waiter's eye. He picked up a menu and a thimble glass of ouzo, and swept up to her, smiling.

She ordered charcoal-grilled lamb and Greek salad, surprised herself by drinking the complimentary ouzo – she never drank spirits at home – and selected a bottle of white wine for the meal. She wouldn't finish it, but it would keep overnight in her apartment fridge.

The family opposite were near the end of their meal. They were British – she remembered them from the flight. A couple, both dark-haired, in their early forties, and two teenaged girls, perhaps thirteen or fourteen, one dark, one fair, very unalike. Strange. In a flash of understanding Helen guessed that she was looking at mother, father, daughter, and daughter's friend, brought along for company. The man was heavily built, overweight, even, thick-lipped and un-smiling. But, acknowledging that she was watching him, Helen acknowledged too that he had an over-ripe, ruined attractiveness.

She smiled to herself and pulled her gaze away. When had she last stared at a man like that? When, last, had it produced such a feeling? As if a bud inside her was threat-ening to open. Just sitting here, staring now out across the sea, she was aware of the sensual pressure of flesh on flesh, where her crossed legs touched at the thighs.

The food and wine arrived and she concentrated on nour-ishing herself. Maybe, she thought, I am still drugged. Maybe this is a life-affirming reaction to the flight. Maybe tomorrow, after a proper night's sleep, the bud would tighten and close again. She wasn't sure whether she wanted it to.

After the meal the music became louder and for a while she watched the waiters dance in a line, arms across shoulders and waists, looking very serious; or perhaps they were shy. Then she took a short walk along the dark beach carrying her half-full bottle of wine. The very idea, she thought with amusement, picturing herself. Eventually she returned to the apartment and sat on the balcony, watching the late-night comings and goings along the beach road and breathing the scented night air. The apartment next door was in darkness, though the balcony rail was draped with towels and swimming shorts. She went to bed before one, and slept deeply.

In the morning she swam in the sea early – before ten – and then dressed in a thin long-sleeved shirt and calf length skirt. Her sallow skin tanned easily but she believed in being sensible. By eleven-thirty she was a hundred yards down the beach road at Denny's Bar, where the tour representative had arranged to meet them. The rep would welcome them to the island, sort out any problems, and try to sell them excursions and hire cars.

About twenty people had collected in the bar. Helen ordered a coffee and sat down. She smiled at the family she had seen in the taverna last night. The woman smiled back and, after a moment, though looking preoccupied, the man did too. Most of the tourists were couples or family groups. The boys from the apartment next to hers were not here. Too early for them.

The young female rep sat at a table in the middle of the bar looking professional and cool in her crisp striped uniform. She welcomed the group and asked if everything was to their liking. This elicited a smattering of minor complaints: light bulbs broken or missing, door catches ineffective, inadequate cutlery. After she had taken details the heavy dark man from the group with the teenage girls raised his hand and said, 'When we booked to come here, we were told these were family apartments.'

The rep kept her face bright and agreed, they were. Mr Brian Carlton, wasn't it?

He nodded. 'There's a group of lads here,' he said. 'Four of them. Other side of the stairway from us.'

Mr Carlton's daughter and her friend were turned away from the tour group. The backs of their heads looked excruciated. The daughter even had her hands over her ears. The mother, Helen thought, looked unwell.

The rep glanced around, checking that the boys were absent. 'They're pot-luckers,' she explained, sounding unapologetic. 'We simply slot them in where we have vacancies. Is there a problem?'

Pot-luckers, Helen knew, got a large discount in exchange for not being able to choose their accommodation. Mr Carlton would know this too; it seemed to incense him more. 'Ha!' he said.

'I'm sorry?' The rep lifted her eyebrows. Helen rather admired her for trying to pin the man down. She guessed the nature of Mr Carlton's problem: the two halves of it at that moment got up and ran off into the sunshine. Everyone heard their escapee giggles.

Mr Carlton shook his head with bad grace and the rep moved on to excursions and car hire. People took their printed price lists and began to wander away. Helen had had no breakfast as yet and ordered a sesame seed cake and a soft drink. The café was very pleasantly located. As she bit into the cake the rep leant over her.

'Miss Lowe, isn't it?' The young woman drew up a chair. 'Can I have a word?' She had a barely made-up girl guide face. Very competent-looking, Helen thought, for someone so young.

'You're next to the boys.' For the first time the young woman's eyes were anxious. 'As far as you know, are they behaving themselves?'

Helen smiled. What bad behaviour could the boys possibly have crammed in, in less than a day? 'I've hardly seen them,' she said. 'Or heard them. No complaints at all.'

The young woman looked relieved. 'I'm sure they're nice boys. The wild ones don't come to Zakynthos. Young men need holidays too.'

'Of course,' Helen agreed. 'I think Mr Carlton is just being fatherly. Girls … well … they can be silly, can't they?'

'The youngest of those boys is nineteen,' the rep said impatiently. 'They're not going to be interested in children.'

'No,' Helen nodded. 'I'm sure you're right.'

They chatted for a while – the young woman knew, of course, that Helen was temporarily on her own, and probably considered it her duty to be sociable – and then Helen strolled around the village looking at the few scattered shops and buying fresh food for her lunches. She'd brought essentials like coffee and tea with her from Britain. Walking back to the block she thought how extremely content she felt. How physically well. The fierce heat seemed to penetrate to the very core of her. Warming and relaxing and loosening. Deep heat, she thought, not remembering where the expression came from, but thinking it summed up the sensation exactly.

Outside the building two of the young men from the corner apartment were standing under the courtyard showers in swimming shorts, washing beach sand and salt from hair and feet. She smiled at them – impossible not to, such energetic-looking young bodies – and said, 'Good morning.' Both boys said, 'Morning,' back with quick smiles, though she was fairly sure that they had no idea who she was, or why she had greeted them.

Up in her apartment she stored her purchases in the fridge, poured herself a glass of cold white wine, and settled herself in a chair on the balcony. From here she had a bird's eye view of activity below: the boys still showering, and their two companions now approaching on the beach road, pushing mopeds. The rep had warned visitors earlier not to hire bikes, because of the danger of accidents on the poorly surfaced roads, but of course the boys hadn't been there. Doubtless they would have ignored her advice anyway – all Greeks, young and old, rode two-wheelers.

Movement by the taverna caught Helen's eye. Two small figures – aha, the young girls, huddled at one of the side tables, behind a mass of pink oleander flowers. Watching – oh incorrigible creatures – the young men shower. Where was Mr Carlton? Helen guessed he wouldn't be far away. There he was, under a sun umbrella on the beach, a solid figure in summer weight trousers and short-sleeved shirt reading a newspaper, a beer bottle and tall glass on the table in front of him.

It would be possible, Helen thought, to sit here all day and be entertained by events below. The showering boys had finished now and were pushing their feet into training shoes. One of the moped exhausts pop-popped into life. Two machines for four boys; Helen wondered where they were going.

It looked as if the young girls were wondering too, with some anxiety. The sight of the mopeds had flushed them out; they were approaching the boys, swinging their bodies diffidently, coyly. The young men had seen them but were pretending they hadn't. One of the girls called out, 'Where you going then?' and had to repeat the question before she got a throw-away reply, which Helen missed under the revving of the moped engines. The two young men climbed on to the pillions and the machines moved off into the road, wavering at first, then pulling more strongly. Then they were gone.

The girls' bodies slumped, every limb dejected. Helen could understand their disappointment, empathize with their sense of thwarted passion. It was this place, this island. This heat. She stared at Mr Carlton. Brian. Just now he cut a lonely figure. Everything she had seen of him, and heard from him, had been negative. And yet. The bud that had awakened last night hadn't snapped shut.

The girls below had a plan B. Their heads were suddenly, urgently, close together; they were counting out money. Now they were walking fast, almost running, under her balcony, into the side entrance of the shop next door. The shop which the rep had told them hired out taxis.

Helen knew with certainty that they were going to follow the boys. Would they tell Brian first? No, evidently not. Within five minutes a dusty black car had pulled up in front of the shop and then was moving off, the girls' faces pale eager flashes behind the driver's seat.

It was not her business. The girls would come to no harm. They presumably travelled around unchaperoned in Britain; a Greek island must be at least as safe. Brian and his wife would have to stop fussing. She wondered vaguely where Brian's wife was, then leant back, sipped her wine, and forgot them.

She had a late lunch and afterwards took to her bed for a two-hour siesta. At five she refreshed herself with a cold-water wash, and then went out. This time she walked round the headland to Laganas: a town of dazzling white-faced low-rise hotels and apartment blocks, gaudy gift shops and disco-bars. A tourist playground much the same the world over, except that here the air was balmy and the sea a twinkling copper-sulphate blue. She walked round a gift shop – full of earthenware plates, leather belts, fancy chess sets and silver jewellery, much of it featuring dolphins. Near the checkout were shelves of mildly pornographic novelties. Statuettes of manbeasts with huge, chest-high erect penises, as thick as their arms. And squat muscular couples, rudely, athletically, copulating. On the bases the word 'Zakynthos' was printed in gilt lettering. The island of brute sex, the novelties seemed to be saying, not romantic love. Yet they seemed strangely inoffensive; merely tacky, and amusing.

She cashed some traveller's cheques and walked slowly back along the beach to the village. Then had a swift dip in the sea, a shower – gracious, she had a swimsuit line already – and put a light robe on. While she was towel-drying her hair she heard raised voices from downstairs. She went out onto the balcony.

Brian was shouting at a small crowd of youngsters in the courtyard: the four boys from next door, and a couple more she didn't recognize. And Brian's own two charges. He was actually holding his daughter by her upper arm.

'Your mother's ill!' he was shouting at her. 'She could do without you buggering off all afternoon!' He wagged a violent finger at the boys. 'And you lot haven't heard the end of this. I've reported you to Miss Bloody Summer Sun.' Looking thunderous, he marched the girls away.

The boys turned to each other in a resentful muttering knot: the unjustly accused denied a chance to defend themselves. Though, from the exasperated shrugs, not caring too much, because it was all a ridiculous fuss anyway. Helen assumed that the girls had only just returned from wherever they had followed the boys to, and felt that Brian's anger with them was justified. Especially if he was having to deal with a sick wife too. Poor man – anxiety did make you bad-tempered. If the boys had been caught in the middle – well, life wasn't always fair.

When she went down later for dinner, however, matters appeared to have become more serious. An even larger crowd was gathered at the edge of the taverna dining area – several families seemed to have got no further en route to tables – and at its centre was the Summer Sun rep. She had both palms raised in a calming gesture, though the protagonists seemed, at least for the moment, to be ignoring her.

'You encouraged them,' Brian was shouting.' They told me. How can you pretend you didn't? You brought them home, for Christ's sake.'

'What d'you want us to do? Leave them there?' The spokesman boy looked furious. Possibly a little panicky too. 'They just turned up. Stupid kids.'

'You're lucky I didn't call the police,' said Brian.

'Now now,' said the rep hastily. 'I don't think we're talking about a police matter. Whether the boys invited them or the girls acted on their own, they were free agents, I think we're agreed on that.'

'We didn't fucking invite them,' the boy shouted.

'There's no need for that,' the rep said.

'One of those girls is twelve,' Brian said nastily. 'You encourage twelve-year-olds to go round with you, do you?'

'Lying bloody twelve-year-old, then,' the boy retorted. His friends nodded vehemently.

The rep was looking very unhappy. It was the word of two young, possibly silly girls against four older, possibly exploitative boys.

Helen felt suddenly lordly, that it was positively her duty to intervene. She was, after all, in another life, a headmistress. She pushed through the crowd.

'Excuse me,' she said. 'I saw the young men leave. From my balcony.' She remembered the exact moment of their departure, and the dejected, crestfallen attitude of the girls. She smiled at Brian as, over many years, she had smiled at so many parents. 'The boys didn't encourage them. The girls decided after they'd gone to follow in a taxi. I saw them, counting money out. The boys had definitely left by then – they can't possibly have known.'

One of the young men at her side murmured, 'You tell

'em, lady,' and another hissed relieved air through his teeth. Brian's hooded eyes blinked at her. The rep's lips were parted as if she was holding her breath. Helen moved towards Brian. 'I expect the girls thought you'd be cross with them. Well ...' she smiled her sympathy, one parent-aged adult to another. 'Who wouldn't be?'

Brian stared at her, then gave a quick tight smile and shook his head, defeated. He'd wanted to believe his daughter and her friend, or perhaps he'd felt he had a duty to; now he was excused that duty. He raised a capitulating hand at the rep; the argument was over.

The crowd loosened. The rep knew when not to flaunt a victory and hustled the boys away. Helen wanted to show kindness to Brian. To take your children's word was laudable, and he'd accepted defeat well. Aware that she was leading him into the taverna, she said, 'And your wife is ill, is she? I'm sorry to hear that.'

'She has a migraine,' Brian muttered. 'She'll be fine tomorrow.'

'Dear me,' smiled Helen. 'What a day. Your wife unwell, the children being thoughtless ...'

Brian sighed and nodded. They were under the taverna canopy now. His face was tired, the face of someone who has had an emotionally exhausting day. He stopped and looked at her. 'I've gated the girls till tomorrow morning. May I ... can I buy you a drink?'

The fact that he was now alone for the evening hung in the air like a tempting, almost too pluckable fruit. Helen barely hesitated. 'Yes. That would be lovely.' She was still brave and confident. The bud within was still unfurled. His wife would be better tomorrow. This would not happen again.

They sat at the same table Helen had occupied the previous night. One drink led to another, and then to a shared meal. Helen, like so many single women, was an expert conversationalist, and Brian was an easy man to draw out. Like popping a cork. An appropriate metaphor, since he was also a prodigious drinker. They had two bottles of wine with the meal – of which Brian drank the lion's share – and several glasses of metaxa afterwards. Brian, Helen discovered, worked for British Rail in some administrative capacity, and was pessimistic about his future. His wife was a radiographer and because they lived in London, where, according to Brian, all state secondary schools were 'rubbish', they were paying for their daughter to attend a private day school. 'Though that's rubbish as well,' he informed Helen gloomily. 'Look at her.'

Helen was aware that their conversation, despite its morose moments, was doing nothing to diminish Brian's attractiveness in her eyes. She had always had a soft spot for vulnerable, moody men. The greatest love of her life had killed himself in a car crash – possibly intentionally – twenty-five years ago. Vulnerable moody men did not make good marriage prospects. However, she wasn't hoping to marry Brian.

After they had watched the waiters dance she heard herself – without giving the words any prior consideration – suggest coffee on her balcony. Brian agreed immediately. They rose and made their way back to the apartment block. Helen missed her footing twice on the outside concrete steps and was for the first time conscious that she had drunk far too much. On the way up Brian insisted on stopping at his own flat to collect a half-full bottle of metaxa.

The moment Helen opened the door of her flat, she knew she had made a mistake. Even the atmosphere seemed to brutally emphasize this; it was like stepping into a furnace. The building's concrete walls, absorbing the sun's heat all day, were now pumping it out into the rooms. There was no breeze and the looseweave insect curtain the far side of her bedroom, glimpsed through the open interior door, hung motionless. Helen switched on the light in the kitchenette alcove and felt a sharp pain stab the back of her eyes. She closed her lids momentarily and when she opened them again, saw, as if for the first time, that she had invited a large, overweight, drunk, sweating stranger into her flat.

She said, 'Go through, why don't you?' trying not to sound appalled. 'I think I'll make some coffee.' What was she doing? She was alarmingly drunk. Brian was even drunker. The heat seemed to make her words fuzzy. But Brian was obeying her, moving slowly into her bedroom, using his left hand to steady himself on the jamb. She reassured herself that he was probably not dangerous. No, it was herself, the reckless, rapacious person she had been up till just a moment ago, who was frightening her.

She busied herself incompetently with the cooker and cups, listening for the sound of the balcony curtain being pulled back, or a chair scraping on the concrete floor, and after a minute or two realized she had heard neither. She moved back from the cooker and peered through the bedroom door.

Brian had made it no further than the nearest bed. He was lying on his back on top of the sheet, his head on the pillow, the metaxa bottle – mercifully still sealed – clasped against his chest. His eyes were closed and his mouth open. The lower two buttons of his shirt were undone, exposing the pale mound of his stomach, a fleshy cushion buttoned by his navel. His jowls fluttered with a bubbling snore.

Helen turned away and rested her hands on the work surface. What a farce. What an idiot she was. Had she actually imagined sleeping with – no, be accurate, having sex with – that man? Saying the words to herself made her conscious of sweat coursing between her breasts. She reached out and switched off the cooker. Her hands were shaking. She didn't want coffee. She wanted escape.

She went into the bathroom and splashed cold water into her face, then held a cold flannel to her neck and to her upper chest above her dress. Then she patted herself dry, picked up her keys and handbag, and left the flat.

Outside the building she looked at her watch. Her hands were steadier. Twelve-thirty. Late for revellers in Britain, still early for Greece. The village was quiet now, the shops dark and empty, but Laganas, she knew, would be hardly into its night-time stride. Many of the discos were advertised as all-night, twelve-till-eight venues. Just as well – she would have to stay up most of the night, if not all of it, if she wanted to be sure Brian was gone before her return. He would wake up, wouldn't he, some time in the night, if only for a pee, realize where he was, and that he was alone, and leave.

She set out, walking slowly and carefully, along the dark beach path. As she rounded the headland she stopped for a moment to gaze at the distant lights of Laganas. A calming galaxy of white lights, studded with clusters of reds and greens. Despite the warmth around her she thought of Christmas. Red, white and green. No orange, she thought; that's what spoils views like this in Britain.

She walked on and after half a mile emerged from the quiet dark into throbbing, music-filled light. Out on the beach the sound level was tolerable. Neat rows of empty sunbeds on the sand forced her inland on to a beachside track.

She reached Laganas' main street, running at right angles to the sea, and turned into it. Sudden cacophony. Motorbikes and cars filled with young people cruised the dusty strip. Music blared. The pavements were wide but cluttered into mazes with rails of beach clothes and milling swarms of people.

Everyone was young, and seemed to know everyone else. The noise level – shouting, laughing, traffic, pounding disco music – was frightening. She was driven on, away from the

beach, by the relentless movement around her. She passed
cafés and bars with empty chairs, but they were still
crowded, hazy with tobacco smoke, and daunting. She
expected to adjust to the noise and crowds, to feel her
heart calm, but instead found her anxiety rising. She had
lost her courage.

She withdrew behind a rail of clothes, out of the human
flow, to catch her breath. She could not walk up and down
here all night. It was hellish. She had felt more comfortable
on the beach. She would return there.

Walking back, as fast as she could, she suddenly realized
that she was thirsty. Desperately thirsty. She had a moment
of panic, imagining herself forced into one of those terrifying
bars out of sheer necessity, and then spotted a small super-
market across the road, still open despite the hour, as most
of the shops were. Huge chill cabinets near the door were
packed with cans and bottles.

With difficulty she crossed the road – some of the motorbikes weaving through the dust had three, even four, youngsters aboard, how dangerous – and safely inside the shop,
bought a large cold plastic bottle of mineral water. At the
checkout she was shocked to see more of those crude man-
beast novelties. Their presence seemed far from amusing
now; more like a nasty, pointed joke. After paying for the
bottle she could not bring herself to break the seal and take
a gulp of water in the shop, though earlier in the day, she
knew, she would have done just that. Instead she clutched
the bottle to her chest, and walked swiftly the last hundred
yards to the relative gloom and emptiness of the beach.

But now what was she to do? She stared around at the
neat lines of sunbeds, the folded sun umbrellas. She was
starting to feel tearful. She wished Margaret were here. Or
some other known, familiar person. Someone to redefine her,
slot her back into herself. She had done something stupid –

something she would never normally have done – and in doing it, cut herself adrift, lost confidence in herself.

She crossed the sand to the nearest sunbed. First, she must quench her thirst. She sat down sideways to the sea, opened the bottle, and drank deeply from it. Then, returning the bottle to her lap, realized that she could see someone she knew. Several of them. Dead ahead, ten or so sunbeds away, was the group of boys from the apartments.

Her immediate impulse was to get up and move away. That, in her present state – she was still, among other things, not altogether sober – they were inappropriate, unwelcome faces. But she hesitated. The boys hadn't seen her. Or, if they had, hadn't recognized her.

And so what if they had. She sank back on the sunbed. She had to be somewhere. She was tired now. Anywhere was better than Laganas main street.

She kept her eyes on the boys. They were larking around, tussling over beer cans. Obviously drunk. One of them ran down to the water's edge – which was astonishingly close, Helen realized, but lapping quietly, so unlike Britain – and started kicking at wavelets. Like a small child, she thought; he was even making sound-effect exploding noises, the kind she heard daily from little boys in her primary school.

Something landed with a dull thunk in the sand beside her. She sat up sharply. It had sounded heavy, whatever it was. A full beer can. Goodness, it could have hit her.

One of the boys, tall and dark-haired, was skipping towards her. His face was turned back to his friends, who were convulsed with laughter.

'That was close,' she said severely, when he was near enough to hear a normal speaking voice.

The boy said, 'Sorry, blame him,' and jerked a thumb over his shoulder at the two behind him. He bent to pick up the can, shouted, 'Catch!' at them, and threw it back.

His apology hadn't sounded remotely sincere: just off-hand, automatic words. Helen watched him run back to his friends, and the tussling resume, and felt stirrings of irritation. That boy had been the group's spokesman earlier in the evening, when they had been arguing with the Summer Sun representative and Brian. When she had intervened on their behalf. He had been close enough now, surely, to recognize her, but it had not occurred to him to either acknowledge this, or thank her. Her annoyance mounted, and although annoyance was not a pleasant feeling it was nonetheless oddly strengthening. It roused in her another self – not yet her true self, but a perfectly possible, credible fifty-year-old self, who was adult and sensible, superior and reproving. She was not a silly, drunken person, as they were, behaving in a silly drunken anti-social way.

She said this again to herself, and realized it was true. What had she done that was so terrible, that she was so ashamed of? That had made her run from the apartment, all the way out here? Nothing. Nothing at all. Foolish thoughts, foolish fantasies, were not the same as foolish deeds. A touch of exotic sun and island beauty had softened and seduced her, made her a little reckless, but where was the crime in that? What were holidays for?

She swung her legs off the sunbed. This was stupid. She would leave now, before another beer can came her way. She would walk back to her apartment and, if Brian had gone, she would drink a pint of water and go straight to bed; if he hadn't, she would simply wake him and send him on his way. If anyone was embarrassed in the morning it would be he, for falling asleep while he was a guest in someone else's apartment, and not herself, as she had done nothing to feel embarrassed about.

She got up and walked away from the sunbed. She had been absolutely right, she realized, in her earlier conviction:

that meeting someone familiar would redefine herself, restore her confidence. But who would have guessed that her saviours would be romping, intoxicated boys? Perhaps, despite their failure to acknowledge what she had earlier done for them, she should now thank them for this favour to her? She wondered how they would respond if she turned back and said, adopting, of course, a pompous, headmistressy tone,'Thanks to your silly behaviour, I am sensibly returning home,' and smiled about it to herself as she strolled back along the beach.

*Also from Honno*

# SILLY MOTHERS

'My neighbour Babs has had them all: Clint Eastwood,
David Essex, Richard Gere, Burt Reynolds …
Not really, you understand. In her dreams.'

Catherine Merriman's first volume of short stories explores
the fantasy, aspiration, sometimes self-deception, that
colour our daily lives: the young mother who finds a face
for her daydreams at the local shops; the 'desperate man'
whose plans for the perfect life are doomed.

*Silly Mothers* was a sell-out success when it first
appeared in 1991. We welcome the opportunity
to re-issue this début collection.

1 870206 10 X                                    £4.95

## About the Author

Catherine Merriman was born in 1949 and brought up in London and Sussex. She studied statistics and sociology at the University of Kent, and in 1970 married her husband Chris. She has had a variety of jobs, including barmaiding, working for the environmental organization Ecoropa and for the Government Statistical Service, but now works as a part-time tutor at the University of Glamorgan. For the past twenty-four years she, her husband and their two children have lived in a hillside village outside Brynmawr in Gwent.

Apart from a 20,000 word novel written at the age of twelve, Catherine did no creative writing until 1985. She has since had short stories published in Welsh, English and American magazines and anthologies. She is the author of three novels: *Leaving the Light On* (Gollancz/Pan, 1992), which won the Ruth Hadden Memorial Prize; *Fatal Observations* (Gollancz/Pan, 1993); and *State of Desire* (Macmillan/Pan, 1996). Her first volume of short stories, *Silly Mothers*, appeared from Honno in 1991.

## About Honno

Honno Welsh Women's Press was set up in 1986 by a group of women who felt strongly that women in Wales needed wider opportunities to see their writing in print and to become involved in the publishing process. Our aim is to publish books by, and for, the women of Wales, and our brief encompasses fiction, poetry, children's books, auto-biographical writing and reprints of classic titles in English and Welsh.

Honno is registered as a community co-operative and so far we have raised capital by selling shares at £5 a time to over 350 interested women all over the world. Any profit we make goes towards the cost of future publications. We hope that many more women will be able to help us in this way. Shareholders' liability is limited to the amount invested, and each shareholder, regardless of the number of shares held, will have her say in the company and a vote at the AGM. To buy shares or to receive further information about forthcoming publications, please write to Honno, 'Ailsa Craig', Heol y Cawl, Dinas Powys, Bro Morgannwg CF64 4AH.